GIVEAWAY GIRL

Victorian Romance

FAYE GODWIN

Copyright © 2024 by Faye Godwin

All rights reserved.

No part of this book may be reproduced in any form or by any electronic or mechanical means, including information storage and retrieval systems, without written permission from the author, except for the use of brief quotations in a book review.

PERSONAL WORD FROM THE AUTHOR

Dearest Readers,

I'm so delighted that you have chosen one of my books to read. I am proud to be a part of the team of writers at Tica House Publishing. Our goal is to inspire, entertain, and give you many hours of reading pleasure. Your kind words and loving readership are deeply appreciated.

I would like to personally invite you to sign up for updates and to become part of our **Exclusive Reader Club**—it's completely Free to Join! I'd love to welcome you!

Much love,

Faye Godwin

FAYE GODWIN

CLICK HERE to Join our Reader's Club and to Receive Tica House Updates!
https://victorian.subscribemenow.com/

CONTENTS

Personal Word From The Author   1

PART I
Chapter 1   7
Chapter 2   19
Chapter 3   33
Chapter 4   43

PART II
Chapter 5   59
Chapter 6   67
Chapter 7   76
Chapter 8   83
Chapter 9   91
Chapter 10   97
Chapter 11   107
Chapter 12   114
Chapter 13   121
Chapter 14   128

PART III
Chapter 15   137
Chapter 16   147
Chapter 17   157
Chapter 18   166
Chapter 19   175
Chapter 20   183
Chapter 21   192
Chapter 22   199

Epilogue   206

Continue Reading...	212
Thanks For Reading	215
More Faye Godwin Victorian Romances!	217
About the Author	219

PART I

CHAPTER 1

1890

Lady Sybil Fallow, Marchioness of Lambert, fussed with her napkin. Her eyes were heavy with the sleep she didn't get the night before. Playing with the food on her plate, her mind was far away. Her appetite had vanished; she could only think of the child inside her. For many days now, she hadn't felt it move. The other three of her lost children all had been moving until the very last minute, so this was different. But her mind wouldn't rest. Was this fourth child doomed like her other poor souls?

Please move, my little one. Mama wants to know you are well.

She placed her hand on her swollen stomach and rubbed it, trying to encourage movement. She had to know it was going to be all right, and not be stillborn like the other three.

FAYE GODWIN

Please Lord, let this child live, and let it be a boy.

"Why aren't you eating? Are you ill?" Lord Irvin Fallow, Marquis of Lambert, and her husband, asked. His was not a gentle tone, but rather irate. Nearly everything she did was not to his approval—ever since their first child was stillborn and a girl.

"I am worried about the child," she said; it was almost a whisper. "I am not hungry."

"Speak up, woman," Irvin boomed, his voice echoing around the breakfast room. "I can hardly hear you."

"It… It is nothing," she said solemnly. She picked up her fork, avoiding the eyes that bore into her. She could feel his cold stare, and it made her shiver in fear.

Her husband didn't say any more and went back to his paper—though, he shook it vigorously to show his irritation. The room was deathly quiet now, apart from the ticking of the clock and the crackling fireplace. The warmth of the fire helped her feel calm and secure; it seemed to be trying to give her a sense of protection of love. It was December, and snow had settled thickly around the estate. When Sybil looked out, it was peaceful, almost as if angels had come to look after her. She sighed quietly; would her next child be a boy as Irvin very much wanted? He had grown quite resentful as each child she had lost was female.

She glanced at the good spread of food, but it was hardly touched. Irvin's plate was still full; he had eaten very little. Her husband was a thin man with a thin moustache, and strong judgment. Sometimes, all Sybil could do was to stay quiet for she didn't want to anger him.

"Stop staring into nothing, Sybil. If you have eaten, leave the table and retire to your room," he said. He put the paper down. "I will be in London for a while. When I am back, I hope you will have a child in your arms, preferably a boy and alive." Scraping his chair back, he stood to address the butler. Sybil began to get up, though the weight of the child pulled her down.

"I would rather not see your swollen stomach. Wait until I am gone."

Sybil felt as if she were slapped. She covered her stomach with her hands under the table.

Irvin told the butler, "Donaldson, have my boxes brought to the carriage, will you? Where is Hilburn?"

"Everything is ready, my Lord," said the butler. "Hilburn is in the hall, ready for you."

"You are going now? You did not say when you were to leave, my love," Sybil said, surprised. She shouldn't be taken aback for he hardly told her anything these days.

"You can hardly expect me tell you everything, Sybil," he said. "You are my wife. You have no need to know everything I do."

Irvin didn't kiss Sybil goodbye, neither did he glance in her direction with a loving smile. No, he simply left the room without a backward glance. Unfortunately, he had been like this for a few years now, cold and uncaring. She wished he was a nicer man like he had been when they first married. He had loved her then. He used to bring her gifts from his travels, take her to the theatre, and dance with her during every season event. But sadly, he had become like a stranger as time went on. She yearned for the man who had once loved her as she loved him.

She felt tiresome now and wished to retire to her bedchambers.

Perhaps, this sleep will do me some good, and the child will move.

She was too fatigued to do anything else. Her lady's maid, Dollie, was beside her as soon as Irvin left, and Sybil couldn't have been more grateful.

"Help me up, Dollie," she said, placing one hand on Dollie's arm and the other on the table. Her back was troubling her. "I wish to sleep, Dollie, but before that, I would like my back rubbed."

"Of course, my lady," said the maid. She looked concerned. "Are you in some pain?"

"Quite so," replied Sybil, and the next moment, she cried out in agony as pain shot up from her stomach.

"Let me get you up to your room rapidly, my lady." The maid walked with her slowly to the staircase. Another wave of pain engulfed Sybil, and she had to stop momentarily. Her hand tightened on the banister as she cried out once again.

"My lady!"

"Help me. I feel I am about to give birth. Quickly, take me to my chambers."

Sybil's heart beat frantically, and she felt feverish all over.

"Let us take her, Dollie," said the butler, coming up behind her.

A footman held Sybil on one side while the butler took her other side. Sybil was tight-lipped as the pain came again, but she allowed the men to help her to her chambers. When they reached the room, Dollie took Sybil to her bed. Mrs. Wilks, the housekeeper, was next to come in.

"We will take care of her from here, Mr. Donaldson," she told the butler. "Perhaps it would be a good idea to fetch the midwife and the doctor. Dollie, bring some warm water and a flannel, we will rub Lady Fallow's back to relieve some of the pain. I suspect the child will not arrive just yet, and perhaps she can sleep."

"You will let Dollie stay with me while I sleep? I do not like to be alone," Sybil asked between tight lips. She knew she shouldn't be so vulnerable in front of the servants, but it was different with her lady's maid whom she had become very close to in the last few years. She wouldn't know what to do without her. In this big house, it seemed Dollie was her main friend and confidante. Sybil told Dollie everything and trusted her with her whole heart; would never repeat their private conversations.

"We both will stay with you," the housekeeper said kindly. "Now, why don't you lie down and sleep. We will have the doctor and the midwife here soon."

Sybil lay her head on her pillow, staring at the ceiling as sweat beads formed on her forehead. She was indeed very hot.

"Have the balcony door open, Mrs. Wilks. I am feeling rather warm." Sybil's voice was faint.

Immediately the door was opened, allowing cold air to enter the room. Dollie arrived with the water and flannel. She undressed Sybil, leaving her in her undergarments. She freed her back and set to rub her down with the warmth of the flannel without delay. Each time a contraction came, Dollie stopped and held her mistress.

Sybil sighed as the cold air soothed her, and she clung to the sensation of the warmth of the rub at the same time.

"I wish to lie on my back, Dollie," she said, feeling the pain shift.

"Of course, my lady." Her maid made her comfortable, covering her with a sheet.

Sybil looked up at the rather beautifully decorated ceiling. Intricate patterns and shapes overlapped into a beautiful picture of flowers and leaves. They seemed to dance. A chandelier supported ornate candle holders; the light from them shining brightly and illuminating the dark blue walls of her chamber. Curious but marvellous paintings hung there, a reminder of the splendid times she and Irvin had spent together on their many excursions, visiting numerous art galleries. These paintings were chosen with care and reason. They'd spent hours conversing about the art in length. Oh, those days had been exciting, indeed.

During the early days of their marriage, Irvin gave Sybil free reign to decorate the house as she preferred, and it pleased her to be useful when he was away. Conducting her research with her friend, Lady Wordsworth, she decided on the decorations and set to have the house furnished.

A rug which was intricately designed and woven, depicting animals, forests, and mountains had been shipped from India. It now adorned the floor of her own chamber, next to the four-poster bed. Drapes which hung around the bed arrived from Spain, and the wardrobe was Parisian.

Sybil turned her head toward the looking glass and gasped. Why, she was distorted like a frail, fading rose, trembling in the rain and wind. It was no surprise then that her husband couldn't bear to look at her. She bit her lip as another wave of pain arrived, and she grasped the bedsheet tightly. As it passed, Sybil fell into an uncomfortable dream.

The wind blew autumn leaves around the graves of her three lost children. The dark clouds released a torrent of rain, and Sybil crouched over them protectively. Long grass covered the graves; Sybil dug it out with a stick. She had no care if her nails became broken and caked with mud, or if her gown became stained.

Her children's names were engraved finely, Elisabeth Fallow, Cynthia Fallow, and Victoria Fallow. Irvin didn't approve of the expense for the dead children.

"I do not see why it is necessary," he said after the headstones were created. "They were not alive when they were born. They had no life. I do not see why you bothered to name them at all."

"It is not their fault they were stillborn," Sybil cried, looking up at the man who loomed from his height.

"No, it was not. It was your fault, Sybil. They died because they were weak girls. If they were boys, they would be strong and alive. How happy we would be if it were so. I blame you, Sybil for your carelessness to not produce heirs to this estate and for my name to continue."

"Do you not care at all for these innocent souls? Do you have no heart?" Sybil asked with wide eyes. "Were they not your children, too? I loved them when they were inside me, and I love them now. They were alive in me."

"I have no care for them. They were your children as you said; they were never mine." Irvin walked away, but Sybil didn't care anymore.

The children were buried under a blossom tree, which flowered every spring. As she now stood under it, blossoms spiralled down to the little ones' graves.

"Oh, my darlings, it is my fault you couldn't live," she told them. "Do not be angry with your father, it was not his fault. Do remember your mama loves you all very much. She will always come and see you."

Sybil sat there in the peaceful silence, not wanting to leave them. The rains had stopped.

Then, she screamed and woke up. Sybil screamed again, writhing in such pain she had never felt before, not even with the last three. The pains came one after the other, and she cried out each time. She saw the worried looks etched on her housekeeper's and Dollie's faces.

"Oh, dear Lord! Make it stop," she whimpered. "The child will not live, will it?" She expected no answer; she knew it already.

Strong hands of the housekeeper held her down, and the soothing voice of Dollie told her to be calm.

"The doctor and the midwife are here, my lady. You are in safe hands," she said.

"Please let my child be alive," she told them. "I cannot bear it!"

Another wave of pain and Sybil plunged into darkness.

"She seems to have fainted," she heard a voice somewhere in the distance. And then, she heard nothing.

"We will take care of Lady Fallow from here," the doctor told Dollie and the housekeeper. "Please leave her chambers. However, we will need many flannels and warm water."

"Is my lady all right?" Dollie asked, wringing her hands in worry. Her mistress was pale as the moon as if she were gone. "Is she alive?"

Everyone looked at Sybil who was very still. The midwife went to check her.

"Lady Fallow has just fainted. She will come around soon. There is nothing to fret about." Her soft voice did nothing to alleviate the worry.

"Let's go down and have some tea," said the housekeeper, placing a hand on Dollie's shoulder. "We can only wait now."

"No, I cannot leave her," Dollie protested.

"Very well, you stay here but wait outside," the housekeeper agreed. "I will have more flannels and water brought up."

With nothing to do, Dollie paced the hallway, hopeful that this child would not be stillborn. What would the master say when he arrived if that were to be true? Would he reject her mistress and marry another woman to bear an heir? What would become of Lady Fallow?

A scream came from inside the chamber. Her mistress was awake. Her heart quickening, Dollie opened the door and was with her immediately. She took Sybil's hand in hers. Sybil's eyes bore into Dollie's, wild as a beast's eyes in hunting.

Dollie had been there with the other three children, and she had seen the pain Sybil had gone through then, only this time, it seemed worse, Dollie feared she wouldn't make it. Neither the doctor nor the midwife asked Dollie to leave this time, the relief to have her there evident on their faces. There was a knock on the door. As Dollie moved to go and open it, Sybil tightened her frail grip, her eyes begging her to not leave her side.

"I shall open the door," said the midwife.

It was a maid with the flannels and water. The midwife didn't allow her to enter the room but took them from her. She closed the door promptly. The night moved on, the contractions becoming stronger and closer together now. Dollie mopped her mistress's brow in a continuous manner and soothed Sybil with soft words. When she could, Sybil drifted back to sleep, only to be awakened again each time a contraction came. She was very weak now and much paler.

Please God, please do not let her die.

"The child is coming," the doctor announced at last. "One more time, Lady Fallow."

Sybil cried out and a small body, still and silent arrived. The midwife took it away and cleaned it, but the child did not cry. The doctor then took it from the midwife, slapping its bottom. Still, it didn't cry. Dollie knew it already; the child was stillborn. Her heart dropped in grief. Her poor mistress... How dreadful of a day it was to be.

"Let me have her in my arms, doctor," whispered Sybil.

"How do you know the child is a girl?" he asked in a gentle tone, hesitant to give the blue child to her.

"I just know," she said. "Please, I need to see her, one time."

The child was placed in Sybil's arms who crooned a tender lullaby to her. Dollie cried silent tears.

"We shall wait outside," the doctor said.

When they left, Sybil turned to Dollie.

"Come to me, Dollie. I have something to request." Sybil spoke in a low voice and told her lady's maid what she wanted.

"The money is in my wardrobe, take it, and give it to the doctor. Explain they must keep this a secret.

Chapter 2

Dollie Askew couldn't believe what Lady Fallow was asking her to do; it was immoral and a lie. She may not like her master, but she didn't believe this was a sound idea.

"Are you certain you want to do this, my lady?" she asked.

Sybil's expression was unwavering; it was indeed what she wanted.

"You are aware I have no choice, Dollie. If Lord Fallow finds out this child was also a girl and stillborn, he will leave me. He will be disappointed once again, and he will detest me for a fourth dead child. What am I doing wrong? Why are not any of my children alive?" Sybil cried, large tears streaming down her face. Dollie sat beside her mistress, who was still covered in blood and sweat.

"Let me get you out of these clothes, my lady, and give you a bath. You will feel much better for it, and it will give you time to think about this," she said.

"I will not change my mind. It must happen," Sybil said stubbornly, like a child herself.

Dollie said nothing. She called a maid and told her to make up the bath for Lady Fallow. A few minutes later, the bath was ready, and Dollie proceeded to take Sybil out of the stained bed and to the bathroom.

"It is not too hot for her lady?" Dollie asked. She tested the water; it was good enough. "All right, leave us."

Dollie helped Sybil into the water and began to wash her. Sybil seemed to enjoy the warmth on her body, and she momentarily closed her eyes. Dollie thought of what her mistress had whispered to her.

"I want this child taken away and buried away from the others. And I want you to find another newly born child and bring her or him to me. I would like a boy, Dollie, but that may be impossible. Offer the woman as much money as she wants. The doctor and the midwife must also know, but they must never give my secret away. I will pay them handsomely."

Sybil suddenly grabbed Dollie's free hand, sloshing water over the bath and onto the floor. Her eyes pleaded desperation, which unnerved Dollie.

"Dollie, I do not know where to bury the child. We must be careful and find a place."

"Perhaps we can bury her in the woods, my lady." Dollie had thought of nothing else since Lady Fallow had given birth. She had a feeling her mistress wouldn't want Lord Fallow to know about the stillborn girl, and she was correct in that thinking. But she was certainly astounded to hear her mistress wanted to purchase a child instead.

"Lord Fallow will not know, and you can visit the child's grave when you want to," Dollie continued.

"Where is ... she now?" asked Sybil.

"She is with the doctor," said Dollie. "Do not request to see her—it will only cause you more pain. Let the poor baby rest where she is."

It broke Dollie's heart to see another child stillborn—was God so unhappy with Lady Fallow? Did she deserve the grief of four dead children? Certainly not. If Dollie had a child of her own, she would gladly give it to her mistress.

Sybil settled back in the water and closed her eyes. Dollie could hear murmurs in the corridor, and she could only imagine it was the doctor speaking with the housekeeper and the butler.

"I shall be back in a little while, my lady. Will you be all right while I speak to the doctor?"

"Yes, and Dollie, I am truly grateful to you," Sybil said, opening her eyes.

Dollie gave a smile, but inside, she was as sad as Sybil.

"Doctor, may I speak with you?" Dollie asked. "It is of a private matter."

The doctor turned to her, his expression as grave as it was when the child was found stillborn.

"It is important, Doctor," Dollie said.

"What is it you want to say that cannot be said in front of the butler?" asked the doctor once they were far away to not be overheard. "Is Lady Fallow all right?"

"She is as fine as she could be, sir. Lady Fallow is quite distraught."

"As she would be," the doctor said. "This is her fourth stillborn, poor woman. I do not know what to tell Lord Fallow."

"That is what I want to speak to you about. You see, it is Lady Fallow's idea to find a newborn child and to bring it to her. She wants it as her own to replace the stillborn."

The doctor's eyes widened in surprise, much like Dollie's had upon hearing such a demand.

"But that is most disgraceful. I do not approve, and I cannot agree with this." The doctor's voice went up a notch. Dollie feared the others would hear.

"Please doctor, do not speak so loudly. My lady is desperate, and she can see no other way. If the master finds out, he shan't be happy with her at all. He could do anything, perhaps even leave her. I do not agree either with what the mistress is proposing, but it may be better for her and the master." The doctor didn't respond. "Lady Fallow is willing to pay you and the midwife a handsome fee to keep quiet. I will take the child and bury her in the woods, far away from the other babies. The master will never know."

"All that may be well, Dollie, but how will you find another living newborn child?"

"I don't know the answer to that, Doctor, but I will go back to my old neighbourhood. I believe I have a friend who may be able to help me."

The doctor sighed heavily. "I still do not approve. It is not right. But if that is what Lady Fallow wants, then I will keep quiet."

THE NEXT MORNING, Dollie carried a small box with the child inside as she and Sybil walked to the woods. Sybil was weak and held onto Dollie to keep from stumbling. Neither of them spoke, but Dollie could feel the grief coming from her mistress like the tide coming in. Her own heart cried tears for the soul of this little girl, and she prayed for her like she had for the others. The trees stood solemnly, watching the women walk around them as if they knew the sadness all too well. Dollie listened to the light rainfall and felt the drops land upon them. It was soothing and it seemed appropriate for this day.

"We are here," she said to Sybil, arriving where the large oak trees gathered in a circle as protective guardians. "We can bury her here." Dollie pointed to a spot beside a large, grey rock. "No one will venture out here, I am certain."

"I have named her Amelia." Sybil smiled sadly.

"Amelia is a beautiful name," Dollie commented, passing the box into Sybil's arms. She stroked the lid but didn't open it. Dollie was grateful for that; it would be much too difficult to see the child wrapped in a white sheet.

Dollie dug the grave as deeply as she could, and Sybil lowered the box down, her tears coming fast. Dollie covered the grave promptly.

"Let us pray for this child to be sent to heaven with her sisters, dear Lord, and may she be happy," Dollie said. She took hold of Sybil's sobbing frame. "Dear God, may you give strength to this woman who has seen much grief. Amen."

They walked back to the house and found Mrs. Wilks standing at the door with a grim expression. Her eyes told Dollie she knew what they had done.

"You will not tell anyone, will you, Mrs. Wilks?" asked Dollie once Sybil was inside her bedchamber.

"I shall not. Her secret is my secret, too," said the housekeeper.

"I am frightened the household will talk, Mrs Wilks. Everyone must be aware the child was stillborn."

"We have contained the situation, and no one will talk. It is forbidden. But what will Lady Fallow tell the master?"

Dollie had no choice but to tell the housekeeper the plan.

"I cannot say I am shocked, Dollie, but it will be difficult to keep the child—if you find one—a secret from the household. Still, I will speak to them when the time comes. For Lady Fallow's sake, we will keep her secret true."

DOLLIE STOOD at the top of her old neighbourhood of Old Nichol Street in Bethnal Green. Rows of slum houses—all identical—displayed the filth and the horrendous stench of litter, urine, and defecation in alleyways. Dollie wrinkled her nose; it hadn't been this bad when she had lived here—had it?

Dollie was only too glad to be away from all this and considered herself to be one of the fortunate ones to have found a job as a lady's maid when some of the women here could only wish for such an opportunity. It was why she decided not to marry and instead look for a reason to get out of there. As she walked down the street, scruffy children marked black with soot played near tin fires. Both burly and skinny men stared at her, grinning wickedly with cigarettes in their mouths, and women dressed in rags hung clothes out to dry on the crooked lines. Dollie narrowly missed a woman throwing rubbish out of her home from the top floor.

"Look where ya going, miss!"

"Do you know if Hattie Kennedy is still living here?" asked Dollie. It had been a long time since she'd seen her old friend, with whom she ashamedly hadn't kept in touch. Dollie was sceptical that Hattie would see her at all. It was a chance Dollie was willing to take for the sake of her mistress.

"She's over there in number fifty-two. You'll 'ave to climb them stairs in your fancy shoes, mind. Look out for the rats, won't ya?" The woman seemed to find this funny.

Thanking her, Dollie made her way across the street and climbed the iron stairs full of rust and dirt, lifting her skirts. As she reached the top floor, she came to a door. No. 52. She could hear many children's voices inside. She knocked.

A scrawny-looking woman opened the door holding a small child in the nook of her arm. She looked fatigued and none too happy to see her. Dollie wondered if Hattie remembered her.

"Hattie?"

"Why you here, Dollie?" She remembered her.

"How are you, Hattie? You look ... well," Dollie lied.

"Go away. I don't care to see you anymore."

"Please. We haven't seen each other for a long time."

Hattie looked at her from top to bottom. "You've become fancy, ain't ya? And your accent changed too, a bit too posh for us over on this road."

"Working at the house has changed me," said Dollie, feeling guilty for leading a better life. But why should she feel guilty? "Look Hattie, please let me talk to you. I need your help."

Hattie began to close the door, but Dollie was quick to put her foot in the doorway.

"I'm sorry for not coming to see you, and I wish I had. I am telling you the truth. Look, I won't take up a lot of your time. But I really do need your help."

"You'd better come in then, but dun't stay fer long."

Dollie stepped into a small and cramped room. There were six children squabbling and running around. A child cried in her cot.

"Hush now," Hattie crooned, putting her other child down and picking the little one up. She seemed to be just born, giving Dollie some hope.

"So, what d'ya want?" Hattie sat on a rickety chair and opened up her blouse to feed the baby.

"You have a fine child there, Hattie. How old is she?"

"I 'ad her last week," said Hattie. "Could do without 'nother one. 'ave too many mouths to feed already." Hattie sighed, watching her child feed greedily from her nipple.

"Well then, maybe you will be pleased with what I have to say."

Dollie explained Lady Fallow's dilemma of the stillborn children and how she was looking for a child to take the place of her last stillborn child.

"Oh, that is unfortunate, but what can I do?"

"Lady Fallow is desperate, Hattie. She would pay anyone handsomely if they gave her one of their children, but the child must be newly born." Dollie looked at the feeding child.

"You want my Sally?" asked Hattie, her expression shocked.

"Lady Fallow will give you thirty pounds. What do you say. Hattie?"

Hattie didn't speak for a little while, and Dollie let the amount sink into her mind. Thirty pounds was a lot of money, and it would help feed her children. She could even afford to move somewhere better.

"Where's Mack, Hattie? I can't see him." Dollie looked around her. "Is he at the factory?"

"Not seen him since Sally came," said Hattie. "'e doesn't matter now. I'll do it, Dollie. I love my Sally to bits, but I 'ave no money, and I dun't know what to do. I will miss her. She is ma darlin' girl."

Dollie was momentarily speechless. She could hardly account for the plan working so quickly. She couldn't believe she would be going back with a child. She could imagine the delight on her mistress's face.

"Move out of here, Hattie. You will be able to do that now. I'll come back tomorrow to take the child and give you the money. But Hattie, you must keep it a secret. No one must know you gave the child away."

"I ain't about to admit to that."

Dollie left Hattie, promising to visit again and more regularly. She would also help in looking for a better house. It was the least she could do in exchange for her kindness. She could only imagine how hard it must be on Hattie to do such a desperate thing.

THE NEXT DAY, Dollie placed the wee sleeping child in Sybil's arms. She was washed and dressed like a child of a lady; no one would have guessed this child came from squalor. Tears sprang from Sybil's eyes as she cradled the child in her arms.

"I cannot thank you enough for what you have done for me, Dollie. I will pay you handsomely for this, have no doubt." A dark thought seemed to cross Sybil's face. "You have told her she has to keep this a secret, and she cannot take her child back? I must know. I cannot bear it if little Charlotte is taken away."

Dollie smiled, "She has promised, my lady. So, this is Miss Charlotte?"

"Indeed, she is. Oh, I am so happy."

The child opened her eyes and began to cry.

"Go on, she wants feeding. The bottle is there. I shall be back when you need me." Dollie closed the door behind her, overjoyed.

Dollie remembered how kind Lady Fallow was to take her as a lady's maid when there was a new position. She had begun as a housemaid and worked hard to get to the top of the ladder of working women. Lady Fallow had done so much for her that Dollie couldn't be grateful enough. She would do anything for her.

"Another girl, but this time she is alive," said Irvin, looking at Charlotte in disgust.

He had arrived from his travels a week ago and was not happy to see Charlotte cooing in her mother's arms.

"Are you not delighted, my love?" Sybil asked, desperate for approval from her husband. "You wanted a child, did you not?"

Irvin gave Sybil a look of utter distaste. "I wanted a boy, Sybil. All I asked for was a living child who must be a boy. And you know very well only a boy can be my heir. I cannot tell you how dissatisfied I am that you failed once again. But there will be more children, and the next time you will bear a boy."

"Dr. Mallingay," announced the butler, stepping aside to let him in. He closed the door behind him on the way out.

"I'm afraid that will not be possible," Dr. Mallingay said. "Forgive me, My Lord, I heard your disquiet in the hall, and I expect the whole household has, too." He raised an eyebrow.

"What do you mean,? What will not be possible?" asked Irvin, his tone sharp.

"Lady Fallow is damaged from inside. Miss Charlotte was a difficult child to bring into this world, and I say she is fortunate to be alive. Lady Fallow cannot bear any more children."

Disbelief passed across Irvin's face. Sybil gave the doctor a small smile, grateful he had kept her lie.

"No, I will not believe it. My wife must bear a boy."

"If you try for another one, Lady Fallow will certainly die along with the child whether it is a boy or a girl. I would like you to take my advice, Lord Fallow, and be happy to have Miss Charlotte."

Irvin looked at Sybil and then at the doctor. He walked out.

"Things will settle, my lady," said the doctor gently. "He will begin to love this child in time."

Irvin didn't bond with the child as the doctor said he would. He kept away from her, dismissing her cries to be loved by a father. He wouldn't look at her and still blamed Sybil for her weakness to bring a 'proper' child into his family. And from then, he hardly stayed at home. Sybil worried that he would never love their daughter as she did, and she could only pray that one day he would. Feeling hopeless, she wondered what her life and Charlotte's life would be like going forward.

CHAPTER 3

SIX MONTHS LATER, Hattie moved into a reasonably sized house away from the squalor and dirt of Bethnal Green with the money she received from Lady Fallow, and she was truly thankful for it. Her home was cleaner than her previous occupancy, and she could take in washing and mending jobs now, too. Yet though being in a better place, she was unhappy. The guilt of giving her daughter away plagued her mind.

The sky was overcast with little sun to show. Hattie threw the stained sheets into the tub of hot water and swirled them around with a stick, her frenzied hair tied up in a bandana. The morning was already too warm, and she was sweating.

"Morning, Mam." Duncan kissed her on the cheek.

Hattie looked up at her eldest son who was fifteen and gave him a small but tired smile.

"Are you going to the shipyard? You look tired as me." Hattie didn't like him working there; it was too rough and dangerous. Why couldn't he find a job at the market? Duncan had been working very long shifts, which had taken a lot out of his body. He was skinnier than she could remember, or had she paid him no attention in the last few months what with grieving for a daughter she had given away?

"My next shift dun't start until later, Mam. I could look after da children for ya, take 'em out for a wee bit."

"Oh, that will do me a whole lotta good," said Hattie. "You're a good boy."

Three-year-old Albert wandered into the side alley and went straight to his mother. She took him in her arms and gave him a big kiss. Albert sucked his thumb and snuggled deeper into her bosom.

"Looks like this one is staying here." Hattie tickled her little one, and he laughed.

"Albert, do you wanna come an' play?" Duncan tried to coax him away, but Albert ignored his big brother.

"Maybe 'nother time." Duncan laughed and then went about his way.

Hattie looked down at Albert, and then at the washing. She really must get on with it; she had lots of it to get through.

"What will I do with you, huh?" She placed him beside her. "Now you must be a good boy like Duncan so I can do my work. Will you do that for me?"

The boy's big brown eyes stared at her, and then he nodded. He looked a lot like his pa who hadn't come back since he'd left many months ago. Good riddance, that was what she thought. She had Duncan, and he was good enough to her; he wouldn't let her down.

As she worked, she thought of her Sally. What did she look like, and did she resemble her? Hattie missed her so much, wishing the greed of the money hadn't taken her and made her weak.

"It's no use feeling guilty," Dollie had said on one of her visits, which were becoming regular. Dollie had kept to her promise to see her often, using her small amount of time off from the estate.

"And it will do you no goo, either. You cannot have her back, and you know that," Dollie reminded her.

Hattie was very aware of this, which saddened her further.

Dismissing the thought of her Sally, she concentrated on the washing, watching Albert at the same time.

DUNCAN HEAVED a long piece of wood onto his shoulder and walked a short length to the other side of the yard, dropping it off. He had a few more to bring back, and then he had to scrub the decks of the ship being built. Men shouted across the yard to each other as they worked on the vast ship. Duncan was used to the clanging, the hammering, and the banging in his head as he walked back to the piled pieces of wood. But he was distracted; his heart was heavy. He thought of his mother's feverish murmurings in the night, which were becoming more frequent and incoherent. He sat down for a moment, putting his head in his hands. Should he ask his mother about them? Was she aware she was doing it?

"Oi! We dun't have time for breaks, and you're not getting paid for no work! Git on with it!" shouted his boss from inside, knocking on the office window so angrily the window shook.

"Sorry, Mr. Callum!" Duncan jumped up, setting back to work straight away. He dismissed his mother's problem from his mind, if only for a little while.

It was becoming dark, and his shift was almost over; he was glad for that. His shoulders were hurting to the point of almost breaking.

"You can't be slacking, boy," his friend and shipyard worker, Alfie, said. "Or they'll let ya off. Somethin' troubling ya?"

"Na," said Duncan too quickly. He didn't want tales of his mam spreading around Bethnal Green.

"If there is, I'll sort 'em out."

"There's nothin' to sort, Alfie. I'm all right, just me shoulder is 'urting."

"Oh, well, better sort that then and quickly. Or the boss'll find another boy to take yer place."

Duncan was very aware of that, and he couldn't afford to lose this job. His mam needed his help in bringing in money with the seven children and herself to feed. Although he did wonder how they were able to rent a better home. He often wondered if his mam had come into money somehow. She never told him ... was that why she was talking in her sleep?

What was his mam so worried about? What was the big secret?

Duncan winced as pain shot up from his arm to his shoulder; hoping no one saw his grimace—but his boss evidently had.

"Leave the wood and do some errands instead tomorrow morning," his boss said. He gave Duncan a list of things to get from the shop. "And 'ave your shoulder seen to. Go home now, boy."

"Yes, sir. Thank you, sir."

Sometimes Mr. Callum was good as gold with him, and at other times, he could be vicious as a dog. It did confuse him.

Hattie's new house stood on top of a small hill, far from the dirty town dwellings, but not too far as to be isolated from everyone. Dollie climbed the steep hill, finally arriving. Clean sheets hung on lines outside, the water dripping from them into pools.

"Good to see you, Dollie." Hattie was outside scrubbing a sheet.

"I see you are busy, I can come another time," Dollie said.

"Na, I want a break. Want some tea?" Hattie asked.

"I would love some."

Hattie dropped the sheet back into the tub and went into the house. Dollie followed, settling herself on a chair as Hattie set about putting a pan of water to heat on the open fire. This was another treat for Hattie, which she didn't have before in the old house. The water was soon boiled, and the tea was made.

"Are you fatigued, Hattie?" asked Dollie. "You are much paler than when I last saw you."

"I miss ma daughter, Dollie. I feel so guilty for giving her away and lying to Duncan that she was ill and died in the night when 'e was at the shipyard."

"It is something you will have to live with now, and that is the truth. It would hurt Duncan if he knew you gave his sister away, and so I think this story is better."

Dollie took to drinking her weak tea. She could sense what Hattie was going to ask.

"I've told you many times. You cannot have her back. Little Charlotte is very happy with her new mother. Please let it be so. Don't cause a problem for Lady Fallow."

Hattie was silent as she drank her tea.

"What is she like? Does she look like me?" Hattie eventually asked.

"She has your eyes and your nose," said Dollie. "She is a sweet child, and the household love her dearly. Lady Fallow has named her Charlotte."

"Charlotte … that's a nice name. But she will always be Sally to me."

"Listen to me, Hattie. She is not yours anymore, come away from that thought. You will only be kinder to yourself if you do. No more talk about Charlotte, and I don't want you asking about her again." Dollie was being harsh, and she was aware of it, but in her mind, she was being kind to her friend.

"You're right, sorry, Dollie... Mack came yesterday. I haven't told Duncan about it."

"He did? Does he want to come back to you?" asked Dollie, surprised.

Hattie shrugged. "He saw how well I live now, and he said he's sorry. I dun't know if I believe 'im. What if he leaves again? I dun't want da children to be used to 'im bein' around and find 'e's gone again da next day."

Dollie placed a hand on Hattie's shoulder. "He might have changed. He might see the wrong he did by you. Why don't you give him another chance?"

"Mam?" Duncan's voice came from outside.

"In 'ere, luv," said Hattie. "Dun't say anythin' to Duncan about 'is father. I'll tell him when I think it's right," she hissed to Dollie.

"Auntie Dollie," Duncan exclaimed.

"Hello Duncan," Dollie said with a smile. "You look well, but tired out. Is the shipyard work difficult?"

"Aye, me shoulder's 'urting too. It'll get better," replied Duncan. He sat down with them. "Dollie, tell me more about da big house, are there any new stories?"

Dollie laughed, "You know I don't like spreading gossip, lad." Then she had an idea. "Duncan, would you like to work at a farm? It is good money. A farmer on the estate is wanting a farm hand. You look good and strong enough to handle sheep and cows and do farm work."

"I like animals, and I dun't care about hard work. I can do it," Duncan said, his eyes lighting up.

"The only thing is you'll have to live on the property because you'll be needed at any time. Animals don't get time off, and they need looking after continuous like," said Dollie.

"No," Hattie said. "'e can't, I won't let him. Dollie, he's all I have got apart from the little ones. I can't look after them without Duncan, and I'll miss him."

Dollie saw the desperation in her friend's eyes and the plea to not take Duncan away.

"But Mam, this would work for us. And I can bring in more money," Duncan said.

"No, Duncan. Maybe you can in a few years when Marigold and Jake are older. I just need you here with me, luv."

"All right. I'll be here if you need me." There was a tinge of sadness in Duncan's voice, and Dollie felt the sadness too, for both Duncan and Hattie.

She hoped Mack would come back and Hattie would allow it, and she wished he would be a good pa to their children. It might give young Duncan a chance to work on the farm. Duncan made an excuse to leave the room and went out.

"Hattie, I have an idea. Let Mack come back to you and see how he is. If he has changed, you will know. And when you believe he won't leave you again, let Duncan work at the farm. This will be good for him, and he won't have to work at the shipyard anymore."

"I dunno, Dollie. I'll think about it."

"That's all I ask." Dollie bid her friend goodbye and made her way back to the estate.

CHAPTER 4

CHARLOTTE GRINNED at her mother as she sat on her new pony, stroking its flank, and patting it with love. Sybil stood next to her, still protective ever since Charlotte had come into her life seven years ago. The warm sun rays caught Charlotte's curly, red hair, and her freckles stood out. She was, indeed, a beautiful child.

"You can ride her for an hour, but then you must come home," Sybil said.

"Why, Mama?"

"Your grandmother is coming today. Do you remember I told you?"

"I forgot, sorry, Mama."

"All right, Jacob will take you around now, but you must be good and listen. I do not want you back in a dress stained with mud."

Sybil watched her daughter trot away with the boy she had hired to teach Charlotte how to ride, and she stayed until she no longer could see them. She walked back inside, as she had to get ready for her mother's arrival. Her mother, Lady Berwick, liked to see her daughter dressed in her finest dresses when she visited.

Sybil remembered the first time Charlotte met her grandmother.

"She is not your child, is she?" said Lady Berwick, looking at Charlotte closely. "She does not look like you…" She turned to her daughter. "And look at the state of you, why are you not dressed appropriately?"

It was true Sybil had lost the will to dress as society expected when her husband did not care anymore. He was away after Charlotte arrived and had not come back until a month later. Sybil was frustrated, perhaps rather irate, with his behaviour. Did he suspect Charlotte was not their child? No, that could not be, for how could he know?

Years had now passed, and still Irvin had not changed his view of the child, and slowly Sybil began to welcome his absence. To be truthful, she looked forward to it.

"Dollie, bring my best dress out. Mama is visiting."

"You do not seem happy, my lady. Do you not wish to see your mother?" Dollie went through the wardrobe.

"Lady Berwick can be tiresome, as you know," said Sybil. "I believe I will need to rest when she leaves."

She glanced at the window. "I hope Charlotte is back before Mama arrives, I cannot stand to see her be disappointed. She would have a thing or two to say about it."

Dollie brought out a blue dress that was newly acquired. "This will look lovely with some pearls around your neck."

"I feel rather a pale peach colour today."

Dollie looked through the collection of dresses again, and eventually found one. She showed it to Sybil.

"Yes. Yes, that is the one. After I am dressed, go and see if Charlotte is back. She will need a change of clothes," instructed Sybil, imagining her daughter arriving in a mud-stained dress despite her warnings.

Unlike other girls her age, Charlotte liked to frolic in the woods, help the stable boy feed the horses, and even feed the pigs at the estate farm. She was not frightened of anything, which alarmed the ladies who came to visit.

After she had changed her dress, Sybil waited impatiently in the drawing room for her daughter to arrive, and when she did, her heart sank. Charlotte's attire was more terrible than she had expected. She ordered the nanny to have her bathed immediately.

***

Sybil sat opposite her mother, who was perfect in every way Sybil was not. Charlotte sat next to Sybil in a clean, yellow dress, and fidgeted. Sybil tried to pat her calm.

"Stop touching your hair, Charlotte," Lady Berwick said, somewhat sharp in her tone. "What have you been doing today?"

"I went riding, Grandmother," Charlotte said. "It was most exciting. We went through the woods, and we stopped to see the squirrels climbing up the trees. It was rather interesting."

"A young lady should be learning to sing and play the pianoforte. She should not be gallivanting in the woods with the servants on a horse. Sybil, I cannot believe you let this happen."

"Mama, Charlotte is a curious child. She likes to do those things," Sybil said meekly.

Charlotte tugged her mother's arm. "Can I leave?"

"Of course." Sybil asked the nanny to take her to the nursery.

"Sybil, I do not approve of the way you are raising Charlotte. You seem to let her do as she pleases. What will she become when she is of age if you allow her to conduct herself with the same behaviour as boys? I pity you, for she will never find a husband."

"Mama, you forget she is only a child," Charlotte said. "I will not have anyone dismissing her goodness."

"Hmph," said Lady Berwick. "Let us talk of something else. Has your relationship with your husband improved? You are aware the ton is talking about his illicit relationships with other women." It was only too clear that Lady Berwick adored Irvin, and she was disappointed Sybil couldn't please her husband and keep him faithful.

Sybil was painfully aware of it. The worst of it was that some of those women had given him a boy. But none of them could take their place as heir of the estate.

"We are as strangers in this house. He still will not spend time with me."

"He is ruining his own life by bedding those women, Sybil. You must make him love you once again and give him a boy."

"Mama, you know what the doctor said. Why do you continue to grieve me so? I was prepared to give him a boy if the heavens would have allowed me."

A stony silence followed as tea and cakes were brought in. But neither woman touched them.

"I must leave, Sybil. I am meeting the charity committee. You have a good day."

This was how it was since Charlotte had arrived. Like Irvin, her own mother was disappointed in her for not bearing a boy. Since Sybil's father died the same year, Lady Berwick's behaviour, as cruel as she was before, had turned even more unappealing. Sybil had never warmed up to her mother as a child or as an adult; she utterly missed her father.

Sybil was secretly glad when her mother left, until the next month when she would come again to see her and Charlotte again, though she had no love for either. Why did she bother at all?

***

SYBIL AND IRVIN waited in the drawing room for the arrival of their visitors, Lord Cecil Calverton, Earl of Burton, and Lady Edith Calverton, Countess of Burton, along with their only son, Dwight. They were one of the prestigious families in Leicestershire. If one was not on their list of acquaintances and friends, they would not be seen as important in society, especially if one's ranking was lower in status.

Sybil twisted her hands repeatedly, uncomfortable in the deafening silence. Irvin ignored her, reading a paper as per usual when he didn't want to speak with her.

To add to the gloom, rain poured from the heavens, blurring the windows. Sybil felt a chill on this summer's day and was grateful for the fireplace, soothing her mind as she gazed into it. She hated the silence.

"Is it not wonderful to see the earl and countess after such a long time?" she said, having had enough of the stillness.

Irvin ruffled the papers.

"Irvin, I am speaking to you. Do have the manners to not ignore your wife? Or is that what you want? Do you not want me anymore as your wife?" she asked plaintively. She wished to snatch the paper away from him and throw it to the floor.

Irvin spoke, startling her.

"Sybil, please do not throw a childish tantrum when we are expecting guests. Calm your mind and be poised. I do not wish to be elevated in grief from this obscene behaviour."

Sybil felt as if slapped. Her heart broke from his cruel words. She was not childish, and neither was she throwing a tantrum. She blinked away the tears.

"Lord and Lady Calverton," the butler came in and announced them.

Irvin put a big smile on his face and stood up as the Calvertons entered. Sybil smiled too, which was painful. She didn't know how she would be able to keep up the charade of being happy for the time they were to be here.

"Lord and Lady Calverton, how lovely to see you," Irvin exclaimed.

"As to you," said Lord Calverton.

After the pleasantries were exchanged, the two couples sat down in their respective seats. Sybil noticed Irvin was rather close to Lady Calverton, and she did not like it at all.

"What a terrible day to arrive," Lord Calverton said with a laugh. "Dwight had no interest in the journey, did you, my boy?"

Dwight fidgeted; he did not seem any better in his temperament even now.

"Dwight, would you like to join Charlotte in the playroom?" Sybil suggested kindly. "She has been expecting you and is quite excited to see you again."

"Oh, may I, Papa?" Dwight asked.

"Perhaps you should stay here with us," said Lady Calverton tightly. "It has been a long journey. Would you rather not rest here in comfort?"

"I have been resting in the carriage, and it was very tiresome, Mama. I wish to play with Charlotte."

"Why not let the boy have some enjoyment, dear? We are on a holiday after all," Lord Calverton said.

"Very well," Lady Calverton concluded.

The nanny was called to take Dwight to the playroom. As they left, Sybil turned her attention to Lady Calverton.

"The season was once again favourable for the ladies; do you not believe so?"

"There were not enough eligible girls coming out to equal the number of boys, which is a shame. Although some of them were most undesirable."

"Lady Annabelle is very attractive," said Sybil.

"I am looking forward to the grand tour once more," Lord Calverton added to the conversation. "I will be taking Lady Calverton and Dwight with me this time. He shall have quite an education learning about the train, the people, and the countries we visit. He very much likes art and history."

"What a delightful boy," said Irvin, a hint of envy in his tone. "If Charlotte was a boy, she would also enjoy the same things."

"But Charlotte is a charming girl. I must say I am quite fond of her. I wish to have a girl as she."

"Charlotte likes to ride and listen to stories of old," Sybil said helpfully. "She is beginning to read well and is quite gifted."

"A girl should have no place in being gifted—she needs to learn to be a lady as she grows," Irvin disagreed in distaste. "If you would stop indulging her in activities suitable for boys, she may even learn to behave as a lady."

"I absolutely agree," said Lady Calverton. "A girl's place is to be in society and be the belle when she comes out. I could not entertain such thoughts of a girl if I had one."

"I do envy you for having a boy," Irvin said.

"A child is a blessing, whether it is a boy or a girl, Lord Fallow," Lord Calverton pointed out. "Do not dismiss the one child you have."

"Quite," Irvin said. He smiled a thin line.

"Should we have some tea? You must be hungry," Sybil said, trying to dismiss the thick air of sudden tension.

"Why not? I feel like some port if I may." Lord Calverton smiled at her.

AFTER TEA, Lord Calverton suggested a promenade in the gardens since the rain had subsided. Lady Calverton decided to stay in the house claiming the chill of the rain was making her rather fatigued. Irvin was also inclined to stay inside.

"Very well," said Lord Calverton.

When he was out of the room, Sybil was alarmed to see her husband leaving his chair and going to sit next to Lady Calverton, and rather closely.

"I believed he would never leave," Irvin murmured seductively into Lady Calverton's ear. Had he forgotten Sybil was still there? She looked away, her face becoming hot with humiliation and embarrassment.

Irvin slid a hand around Lady Calverton's shoulders and kissed her cheek, while she laughed flirtatiously.

How dare he act like this in front of me! Does he have no shame?

Sybil walked away, tears building in her eyes. She ran to her bedchamber and threw herself down on the bed, flooded in tears.

"LET US GO TO THE STABLES," twelve-year-old Dwight said to Charlotte the next morning after breakfast. "I wish to see the horses."

Charlotte was delighted that her second cousin was keen on horses, too, and agreed readily. "We must be quiet," he said. "We do not want to be noticed, do we?"

Charlotte, quite excited, tried to keep calm. Dwight took her hand, and they tiptoed out the front door when the hall was empty. The nanny was in Charlotte's bedchambers preparing her dresses, assuming the children were playing in the playroom amicably. At last, the children arrived at the stalls.

"What are you doing here?" asked the stable boy. "Where is your mother, Miss Charlotte?"

"She is coming," lied Charlotte.

"And your nanny?" the stable boy did not seem to believe her.

"She is coming, too. This is Dwight, and he is my cousin. He is older, so he can look after me."

"Very well, Miss Charlotte," the boy said. "But you must behave. I want no trouble."

"We would like to see the horses." Charlotte put on her pleading voice that no one could refuse. "Especially Prince Henry. Dwight, he is a good horse, and he will like you."

"You have named him Prince Henry?" Dwight asked, smiling.

"Yes, does he not look like a prince?" Charlotte giggled. "He and I are friends and sometimes Trevor will let me sit on him. But I cannot ride him yet, I am too small."

"Soon, you will be tall as I," Dwight said, amused.

They stroked the horse and talked to him, and then they went to see the other horses and ponies. The stable boy let them give the horses apples to eat and allowed them to comb the flank of one of them. The morning wore on, and no one seemed to notice the time until Irvin arrived, angry and flustered.

"Here you are!" he bellowed. "We have been looking for you everywhere. How dare you leave the house without the nanny and without asking us, Charlotte. Dwight's mother is worried sick and will be very upset with you, and I do not blame her."

Irvin took her arm, pinching her skin.

"Ouch," cried Charlotte. "That hurts, Papa."

"Let that be a lesson!"

"Where have you been?" Lady Calverton demanded of her son. "And how dirty you have become." Her look flashed to Charlotte who was now crying and cowering behind her mother. "This is your doing, is it not? You have led my boy astray. He would never do such a thing back home."

"Mama, it was not Charlotte's fault. It was I who suggested we go to the stables. I wanted to see the horses."

"Do not make Charlotte cry, my dear," said Lord Calverton anxiously. "They are only children, and you must let them play. Charlotte, dear, do not be upset. Now, come along with me. I have something to cheer you up. You come, too, Dwight."

"Where are you taking them? I have not finished," Lady Calverton cried.

Lord Calverton ignored her and took the children away. Moments later, he came back with a smiling Charlotte and Dwight.

"What is this?" Sybil asked her, crouching beside her daughter. She took a wooden horse from her. "Is this a gift from Lord Calverton?" Charlotte nodded and once again, hid behind her mother.

"I have decided we shall leave tomorrow morning," Lady Calverton announced. "I cannot let my boy be influenced by your daughter. Dwight, you will no longer play with the girl. Come away with me now."

Lord Calverton pleaded his wife to be reasonable, but she was not listening. She ordered for their boxes to be packed. Irvin gave Sybil and Charlotte a scathing stare.

Later, he started in once again. "This is your fault and that of the child! If she had behaved, the Calvertons would not have left earlier than planned."

He stormed out of the room leaving both mother and daughter in misery.

PART II

CHAPTER 5

"Nimble fingers, Lady Charlotte, nimble fingers." The governess rearranged Charlotte's fingers on the pianoforte. "A lady must play a musical instrument in a delicate manner."

"Why does it matter so?" Charlotte asked.

"You are now sixteen. There will be many suitors looking for prospective girls to court." The governess lifted Charlotte's chin. "And you, my dear, will be one of them. They like ladies who play the pianoforte finely, who can sing in a wonderful voice, and who are polite and courteous."

"I will never court or marry," said Charlotte, looking out the window. "It is quite a tedious affair. I have seen my parent's relationship, and I do not like it at all. I do not want to be dictated to by a man who does not love me."

The governess sighed and closed the lid of the pianoforte. "Let us go outside to the gardens. I believe we can stop practicing today. It is a lovely day, after all."

The sun was shining brightly, the sky had a light blue hue, and Charlotte heard the birds singing. The last few days had been horrible with rain and wind, and she hadn't been able to ride her horse, which she missed very much.

A few minutes later, Charlotte walked down the staircase toward her governess, who waited at the door. Charlotte walked tall and with poise as a lady should walk, bringing a smile to her governess.

The housekeeper, Mrs. Wilks smiled as Charlotte passed her. Ever since Charlotte could remember, the household staff had been very kind to her, and she felt they were family. But that way of thinking was looked down upon. Her grandmother told her she must refrain from becoming familiar with the working class as they were merely servants. But Charlotte ignored her grandmother; she always felt she was different from the people of high society, like she was never one of them. She wondered why that was.

"You are promenading very well, Lady Charlotte," the governess complimented her. "I am very pleased."

Charlotte smiled, and the two women proceeded to the garden.

"Miss Granger, will you marry some day?" asked Charlotte as they approached the manicured flower beds and the trimmed bushes.

"That is a personal question, Lady Charlotte," said the governess.

"Will you answer it?"

"All right. I believe marrying is not a possible option for me. However, I like being a governess. I like teaching young girls to be the ladies society expects." Miss Granger smiled.

"You seem melancholy," Charlotte observed. "Why is that?"

"It is not for you to be concerned about, Lady Charlotte. Let it be," Miss Granger said. But Charlotte wouldn't let it be.

"I may be young, but I would like to believe I am wise. Mama tells me I am wise beyond my years. Please do tell. I will keep it a secret if it is one. I believe you were in love once."

The governess looked at Charlotte dearly. "It was a few years ago when I did fall in love with a man. His name was David. He worked on a ship, and I would not see him for long periods of time. One day, he never came back."

"What happened?" Charlotte asked, intrigued.

"David was to accompany his ship's crew on a voyage to West Africa. When they left Southampton, he gave me a necklace to remember him by. I told him I did not need it because I could never forget him." The governess stopped, perhaps thinking about him. Then she began again. "They were sailing toward the coast of the continent of Africa when the weather turned, and they found themselves to be in the middle of a rather treacherous storm."

Charlotte gasped.

"I was told David did everything he could to save the crew. In the end, he too was lost at sea with the many of them."

Tears pricked Charlotte's eyes. "What a melancholy experience. I cannot bear to think of the anguish you have felt." She noticed the necklace around her governess's neck.

The governess saw her interest in the necklace she wore and smiled. "You are correct in thinking it is the one David gave to me. I loved him with all my heart, and I still do. So, I believe I will not marry anyone else. That is my story. However, it shall not be yours. You will meet someone who will love you, and you will marry."

"And I believe you will also love another man, Miss Granger. And you, too, will marry," said Charlotte taking her governess's hand.

Charlotte admired her governess and believed she was fortunate to work as she did and be independent. "I would like to work one day as an artist or perhaps write books," she declared. "I do not believe I will marry young. How awful it is to be confined to society rules and etiquette, to be at a man's beck and call, to bear children. I cannot do that, not yet. Perhaps when I am twenty."

They came to a bench and sat down. Charlotte lifted her face to the sun, enjoying the warmth.

"Well, before that, you are required to attend balls and parties when the time arrives," Miss Granger reminded her. "Then, you can decide."

But Charlotte was decided that she would not marry young, even if she fell in love. Her suitor would have to wait for her if he wanted her. Her parents and her grandmother would not like it, but she had no concern for them regarding such a personal matter.

※

IRVIN STRODE into the drawing room and stopped upon seeing Charlotte sitting there.

"Papa. How were your travels?" Charlotte asked.

"Never you mind. Why are you sitting here, wasting time? Should you not be with your governess, learning?" he snapped. Charlotte, used to her father's demeanour, didn't flinch at his harsh words.

"Miss Granger has the afternoon off," said Charlotte.

"All your mother's doing, I suppose. I do not recall authorising leave."

Charlotte refrained from reminding him he was hardly at home to make such decisions. He was hardly at home to sit and converse with her, either. She bit her lip.

"Papa, I would like some more books," she finally said.

"Do we not have enough books?" Irvin went to the drinks cabinet and took out a bottle of whisky and poured himself one.

"I would also like more parchment, ink and quills,"

"Whatever for? Do you intend to be a scribe?" He laughed in a cruel manner.

"No, but I would like to write poems, perhaps even a novel. I find it quite fascinating. I read a book about a—"

"I do not care what you read, Charlotte. You can have what you've requested. Now leave me, for I want to be alone."

Charlotte wished her father wouldn't dismiss her so; she longed for his warmth and love, which she never obtained. She asked herself again and again why this was so; she even asked her mother. But she never got an answer.

Charlotte slipped out of the drawing room and went to her mother's chambers where she was resting. She laid down next to her, taking her hand in hers.

"Charlotte? What is the matter?" Sybil asked.

"I feel alone and melancholy, Mama. I don't know what to do." Charlotte searched her mother's eyes. "Will Papa ever love me, or talk to me as other fathers do with their daughters?"

"Your father loves you very much," said Sybil, kissing Charlotte on the forehead.

"That is not true, and you are aware of it. But do not concern yourself, Mama. I shall let you rest now. I do hope you feel better soon."

For a few months now, Sybil had been ill. The doctor did not understand what was causing her to be weak, sometimes to the extent that she was not able to eat. Irvin didn't seem to care. One day, she had overheard her father say that it was her fault her mother was tired.

Charlotte didn't understand what he was talking about. When she asked her mother, all she did was cry. Charlotte decided to never ask again. She left her mother to rest and took to the stables where she could talk to her horse. He listened attentively and was her friend. And then later, she wrote to Dwight, who was fortunate to be studying at university.

I wish I could go; how amusing and entertaining it would be to learn from scholars.

However, she knew it was not possible for a lady to attend such places; their place was to marry and have children, was it not?

Her present horse, whom she named Fabian, neighed on her approach. She embraced his next immediately, stroking his flank.

"How would you like to take me for a ride, Fabian? I am certain you are as bored as I am."

The horse neighed as if agreeing. Soon, Charlotte was galloping away from the estate, the wind in her hair. She didn't care who saw her. If she was discovered she would be scolded. She had no fear or that, for now, she was free.

CHAPTER 6

CHARLOTTE DREW BACK the curtains of the window of her bedchambers. She watched Dwight disembark the carriage with his father. Her heart fluttered seeing him after a long absence. She found him to be most attractive. What would he say when he saw her? The last time she saw him was two years ago, and she had grown since then.

"Where is my dearest Lady Charlotte?" came the jovial voice of Lord Calverton from the hall. "I am keen on greeting her."

A very excited Charlotte started down the stairs at a run, but calmed down to a walk mid-way as she observed Cousin Calverton and Dwight standing in the hall. Irvin gave her a stern look to behave like a lady.

"Cousin Calverton." She curtseyed. "How do you do?" Charlotte glanced at Dwight, who grinned.

"Let me look at you, my dear. Oh, what a beautiful lady you have become. Lord Fallow, you must be so proud," said Lord Calverton.

The group moved into the drawing room. Charlotte sat next to her nervous mother, who looked rather frail today even more so than yesterday. Charlotte was secretly glad Lady Calverton wasn't there.

"Lady Calverton sends her good wishes. She couldn't come due to an illness. Nothing to worry about, it is just a mere cold," Lord Calverton explained.

"We are glad to have you here," said Charlotte. "Is that not so, Mama?"

"The Calvertons are always welcome," said Sybil. "It is a shame Lady Calverton is not here to enjoy this part of the country."

"And how are you, Mr. Calverton?" asked Irvin. "I hear you are soon to move to Germany?"

"You are correct to hear it, Lord Fallow. I will be working for Frederick Bauer in Munich as a solicitor. They are very well known in England and the rest of Europe," said Dwight.

"And so they are," agreed Irvin. "May I extend my congratulations. You will learn well, and become accomplished, I am sure."

"I believe I shall have to excuse myself, Lord Calverton," said Sybil. "Do carry on. Charlotte, would you assist me to my bedchambers?"

"Very well, Mama," said Charlotte. One glance at Dwight told her he wanted to spend time and converse with her.

"And then perhaps Dwight and Lady Charlotte can go for a ride?" Lord Calverton suggested. "My son has requested it, and I am certain you two want to converse." He looked to Charlotte as a loving father, and Charlotte gave him a smile.

She wished her father was like him.

※

"I believed we would not be able to get away and be alone, Lady Charlotte," said Dwight.

"Lady Charlotte? When have I been Lady Charlotte to you? You call me Charlotte, do you not?" She smiled shyly as they stood with their horses at the stables, ready for an adventure.

"You look very much a lady now, Charlotte. You are no longer a child," Dwight said, his eyes boring into her. Charlotte felt herself blushing.

"You have grown too, and you have a moustache," she said. "It is quite strange to see you like this."

Even though they kept in touch by letter, seeing him again was rather exciting. Charlotte didn't expect to feel differently with him. But the days when they played together were not going to be the same anymore.

"Shall we ride?" he asked eventually.

"Indeed."

They trotted amiably along the path, leading away from the estate. As they rode past the gate, the horse reared on his hind legs, almost throwing her off. A passing man, with a startled look, fell to the ground. They stared at each other.

"Look where ya goin', lady!" he said, jumping up and dusting down his clothes.

"I do apologise," said Charlotte. "It was my horse; he was surprised. You promenaded across us."

"Do not blame me for walkin' where I wanna." The man narrowed his eyes. "You look like someone. 'ave me met?"

Dwight laughed. "I very much doubt it, she is a lady. You would not have seen her where you live or anywhere else for that matter. Come along, Lady Charlotte."

"Please, forgive me," Charlotte said to the man again, feeling guilty and confused. She was certain she had not seen the man before, but why did he seem so familiar?

"Is something the matter?" asked Dwight.

"No, nothing to fret about. Shall we carry on? Tell me more

about your new adventure to Germany. You did not mention it in your last letter."

"It all happened as a surprise, really," said Dwight. "After university, I was invited by the Dean to a gathering at his house. He introduced me to many people in the law industry, and one of them was a Mr. Frederick Bauer, a rather charming and intellectual man. We conversed well and at length, and before I knew it, I was invited to apply for a position at his company in Munich."

"How excellent," said Charlotte. "I am certain it would be a rather fabulous time for you. However, I do hope you will come home regularly."

She wanted to see more of Dwight and would miss him dearly. Germany was a very long way away. "You will not stay away for two years as last time, I dearly hope."

"I shall not, for I am also keen on seeing you, my dear Charlotte."

She glanced at him sideways. A strand of long hair fell across one eye and sun rays captured the colour of his pupil. He caught her staring at him, and she quickly looked away.

"When do you believe you will be going?" she asked.

"In a week or so. Mama is not so happy about it. She would like me to find a wife and marry before I settle down. However, I do not wish it so yet."

"Why not?" Charlotte asked softly.

"I want someone that I will love, and I have not found her yet. And I would like to be working first. It is what I desire. As you know, my brother will inherit the estate, and therefore I shall not. I will need to bring in my own income."

"Well, I believe it is very desirable for a woman to know her betrothed is earning well. I am certain you will find a woman to meet your wishes very soon. If I had a choice and could work, I would not hesitate for a moment." That caught Dwight's attention.

"How interesting. What would you do if you were to work?"

Charlotte told him of her wish to be a novelist or an artist.

"I cannot decide which one, perhaps both. If I were to choose, oh, it is difficult... Perhaps I would take up writing where I could lay out my heart on the pages of a novel. I perhaps could illustrate it, too."

"You are a rather a forward-thinking lady. I am impressed," said Dwight.

Charlotte was happy to hear his approval, not that she was looking for it.

"Have you spoken to your father about this?" he asked.

They stopped at a stream and dismounted from their horses, leading them to the water for a drink. The quiet babble of the stream calmed Charlotte as she spoke.

"Father would never agree to my wanting to work," she said. "If he had it his way, he would have me married now. I must be grateful he had not shown much interest yet in such an idea, and I can be a free lady."

They sat down on the grass. Dwight knew about the difficulties she had with her father, but he never probed further about her feelings about it. Charlotte was grateful; she didn't like to think or talk about her ill relationship with him.

"If I may say so, your mother does not look so well. Is she rather ill?" he asked.

"It is not something I like to put in a letter." Charlotte picked a buttercup from the earth and twirled it around her fingers. "Mama has been ill for some time, and I worry. The doctor does not know the cause."

"I do wish I could do something to help," Dwight said with honesty in his tone. "Perhaps I can ask my doctor to see her? He is very respected."

"That would be lovely, Dwight, if you could," said Charlotte. "But Papa will not agree to such kindness. He is a stubborn man who takes a lot of pride in his own resources."

Her eyes filled with tears. "Papa blames Mama for her ill form. I do not understand why or what to do."

Dwight took both her hands and looked deeply into her eyes. "All will be fine; you must believe it."

Charlotte pulled her hands away and looked around them in fear.

"Someone could have seen us, Dwight. I do not even have a chaperone." She stood up hurriedly.

"I apologise. I was not thinking. Oh dear, do not think badly of me, Charlotte."

"We must hurry home. I do not want anything else to happen."

Without further delay, they galloped back to the house. Charlotte hoped her father would not notice her and Dwight's long absence. She was the first to enter the house.

"Where have you been?" Miss Granger took her away from the hall. "Were you with Mr. Calverton? Did you have a chaperone?"

"I did not. Do not think terribly of me, Miss Granger. Dwight, I mean Mr. Calverton is a friend of mine, and we have known each other since I was a child. He would do no harm."

"Well, it is a good thing your father and Lord Calverton did not miss the two of you."

"Where is my father?"

"They are having rather a jolly old time in your father's private room, I believe."

"And Mama?"

"Lady Fallow is resting. I was told to keep an eye out for you, and I was beside myself as I couldn't find you."

"I am sorry, please forgive my foolishness." Charlotte felt guilty for her selfish adventure, not thinking about the consequences of her ill actions.

"Lady Charlotte, you must remember you are no longer a child. You are a woman, and he is a man. Wherever you go with a man, you must have a chaperone in attendance. I believe I have informed you of this."

"You will not tell my parents, will you?"

"Of course, I will not. But do be careful, Lady Charlotte. I cannot hide your adventures forever."

CHAPTER 7

AFTER DWIGHT LEFT FOR GERMANY, Charlotte was distraught by his absence. She had enjoyed his last visit and was grateful no one had reported their little unchaperoned adventure. If she closed her eyes, she could still feel his hands on hers, and her heart pounded. It was an unusual feeling, one of delight and hope of good things to come. She felt happy, something she hadn't experienced in a long time. Why did she feel so happy and light when Dwight was here with her?

"Charlotte?" Sybil said. "What is on your mind, my dear?"

Charlotte hadn't realised she was so deep in thought. "I was thinking about Mr. Calverton. He is fortunate to be travelling to Germany and working, do you not think so?" Charlotte threaded a needle into the fabric.

"I suppose, yes. I have seen him grow from a boy to a man, and I find it quite endearing to see him become so fruitful in his work practices. He will become a good husband to someone, I am certain of it," replied Sybil.

"He told me he will not marry yet."

"Well, he is mistaken. When he meets the one he loves, he shall."

"Mama, did you love Papa when you married?"

"Very much so, my dear." There was a look of surprise on Sybil's face.

"And do you love him now?" Charlotte asked. Sybil stopped smiling. "Why is he angry with you all the time, Mama?"

"I still do love your father. But you must not worry about such things. You are too young to understand. It is not unusual for a man and his wife to have disagreements now and then."

"Then I shall not marry," Charlotte said pointedly.

Sybil set down her sewing and went over to Charlotte. "I believe you will change your mind, just as Mr. Calverton will. Do not upset yourself over your father's temperament, it is not his fault he is the way he is. And not all men are like him. There was a time when he loved me very much, but then something happened, and it changed him."

"What happened?"

"Now is not the time to tell you, my sweet Charlotte. Let us continue with the sewing, and then I shall rest again."

Charlotte watched her mother pick up her work, but she was not with her now. She had withdrawn and was very melancholy. Charlotte wanted to ask her about the incident that changed her father, and thus made her mother so undesirable to him. However, she couldn't ask her mother again for she didn't want to upset her anymore.

She looked down at her embroidery work. The image of the flower seemed as forlorn as her heart; its loneliness echoing her own.

"IT IS SO good of you to call, Lady Fallow. And Lady Charlotte, how beautiful you are in your splendid dress. I have not seen one like this, where did you acquire it?" asked Lady Wordsworth, Sybil's neighbour and friend.

"Mama ordered it from the shop in London. It is Parisian," said Charlotte.

They were sitting in Lady Wordsworth's parlour, which overlooked a stunning lake and distant hills. Tea and sandwiches were laid on the table before them, yet untouched.

"But Sybil dear, you look quite ill. Please do tell, it is nothing serious?" Lady Wordsworth asked.

"I am recovering from a recent illness. It has sadly altered my appearance," Sybil admitted. "The doctor had advised rest and good nourishment."

"Then, you must eat. Fill up your plate and have more tea."

Across from Charlotte sat her friend and Lady Wordsworth's daughter, Anne, who smiled at her.

"Mama, can I and Lady Charlotte be excused?" she asked and turned to Charlotte. "Dearest, would you prefer the gardens? They are in bloom, and I am excited to show you how wonderful they are."

"You two girls go," said Lady Wordsworth. "Perhaps you can have tea outside."

"That would be lovely, Mama."

CHARLOTTE AND ANNE promenaded among the flowers and shrubs as footmen set a table and two chairs on the lawn. Tea, cakes, and sandwiches followed. A bumblebee flew over the flowers, its wings composing a soft buzzing sound. The girls watched it fly away as if in a trance, and then it disappeared around a bush. Anne entwined her arm through Charlotte's.

"It is so good to see you, my dear. And how beautiful you have become," Anne declared.

Charlotte laughed, "I find a lot of people are saying that to me. My governess, Lord Calverton, and his son, Mr. Calverton. I don't know what all the fuss is about. I am still Charlotte, am I not?" Charlotte looked down at herself. "I see no difference."

"Perhaps you do not, but other people have seen it. Dearest, you have developed into a fine, young lady. You are more beautiful than most of the young women who have been promenading about lately. And if I were a man, I think I would like to court you."

Both of them laughed at this.

"Tell me about this Mr. Calverton," said Anne. "Is he handsome and charming? I do not believe to have heard of him or met him at any balls."

"Mr. Calverton and I have known each other for many years—since I was a child. He is quite a private man and does not attend many social parties, if I am correct. Lady Anne, may I tell you a secret? It is something close to my heart."

"Do say, I am rather intrigued."

The ladies circled back to their tea and sat down. Anne dismissed the footmen and poured the golden tea from the painted teapot. Charlotte took a cake from the delicate stand.

"I am in confusion. When Mr. Calverton visited me recently, I experienced some unusual feelings in my stomach and in my heart. I felt myself become warm with one glance from him.

What is this? Is this love? I have read many romance novels, but I have never experienced it." Charlotte was aware she came across as naïve, but she had to be certain what she was feeling was true.

"Oh, my dearest Charlotte. You are indeed in love," her friend exclaimed. "And what a lovely time it is for you, is it not?"

"I am unsure. Mr. Calverton has left for Germany, and I shall not see him for a long time." Charlotte fell silent for a moment. "I cannot write what I feel for him in a letter. If someone else read it, it would be rather scandalous. What would Mama and Papa say? I cannot think of anything worse than this."

"You must not fret about such things, my dear. And there is no hurry to tell the man tales of your heart. As you say, he is in Germany, and you are here. When you come out in society, there will be other men who will be wanting your attention. You will forget about Mr. Calverton. However, I am delighted that you have realised what love is." Lady Anne sipped her tea and bit into a sandwich.

"Have you fallen in love?" Charlotte asked as she lifted the tea to her lips.

"A man has been courting me, but I do not believe I am in love with him. He is a nice man, honest and kind, and he is a respected member of society. I met him last spring, and we have danced together at many balls. I have a wonderful time, as will you when you dance with prospective candidates. I believe I have yet to meet the man whom I will love."

"And will you marry if one proposes?"

"Only if he is worthy of my respect."

ON THE WAY HOME, Charlotte thought of her conversation with Lady Anne. She was now in a better mind knowing it was love she felt for Dwight, but with her happiness also came melancholy, for she wouldn't see him for some time.

Would he find a woman in Germany and love and marry her? Would he bring her to England perhaps, and how would Charlotte feel about it?

I admit I do not like that prospect at all. It is selfish of me certainly, to want to claim him when he is so far away from me and is on a new adventure where he will meet other women. I am young. I must calm my heart. Love can wait. I must concentrate on my education and my wish to be a writer and an artist. Yes, that is what I shall do.

CHAPTER 8

THE GENTLEMAN'S club was busy with ladies of entertainment and men who came to have a jolly time, away from their wives and families. This was also true for Irvin. He sat alone this evening with a port in his hand. He disliked his life and what the future held for him and his estate, for he had no heir to pass it on to. All because his wife could not bear a son.

It didn't matter how many women he slept with or how many parties he went to alone. It mattered not to him that he had fathered boys with these other women, who could never be his heir. He chose to have many adventures and relationships to drown his sorrows. He embarked on many travels. But nothing allowed him happiness.

He still had an estate to look after, a wife he did not love, and a daughter whom he had no heart for. She was useless to him.

Yet, they pined for his love, which he couldn't and wouldn't give.

"Lord Fallow, I thought it was you," Lord Calverton's voice boomed above him. He immediately took a seat opposite Irvin.

"Lord Calverton, I had no idea you would be here," Irvin said. He disliked the man for adoring Charlotte and making him feel inferior on his last visit. "Are you here on business?"

"Not quite. My wife and I have been travelling since Dwight moved to Germany. We feel his absence greatly. And with his older brother in America for a while with his family, the house is too empty without them."

"How is Lady Calverton?" Irvin asked, although he did not care one way or the other. "Was she not ill previously?"

"She was, and now she has overcome the cold." Lord Calverton stared at Irvin, unnerving him. "Tell me about your wife. I hear she is gravely ill."

"She is well enough," came Irvin's curt reply.

"Forgive me for saying so, but I feel you are not doing what is right for your wife and your daughter. I have observed the way you behave toward them, and I must say I am alarmed. What have they done to receive such punishment from you? Word has spread that you have done some undesirable deeds, which I do not wish to repeat here." Lord Calverton's eyebrows lifted. "I do feel pity for such a man to succumb to this."

"I have no heir, Lord Calverton, and Charlotte is useless to me. I wanted a boy, which I never received from my wife. So, do not give me your opinion on what I should and shouldn't do. What I do outside of my estate is my business, and I want to keep it so. Do leave the table now, Lord Calverton, for I will regret what I will say next if you stay any longer."

Behind his simmering fury, Irvin watched Lord Calverton leave, shaking his head as if he indeed did pity him. Irvin banged his glass on the table, spilling some of the port and alerting others around him of his temperament. They moved away.

"Yes, leave me alone, all of you," he shouted, and then he stormed out of the club.

"Why will you not look at me, Irvin?" Sybil asked, her forehead pinched with pain. "How can I please you?"

Irvin glared down his glass of port. "You ask me if you can please me?" He laughed. Irvin knocked down his port and poured himself another one. "I have nothing to say to you."

"We do not converse anymore. I do not know where you go and when you will come back. We are strangers in this house. Why will you not share your love with me and with your daughter?"

"Charlotte is *not* my daughter," he sneered. "She does not look like either of us. I do not have any love for her as I do not for you anymore, Sybil. I cannot stand to be in the same room as you, for your appearance disgusts me. You are not the attractive woman I married. You are sick all the time." He straightened his cravat. "I have decided to stay in the country house, and therefore I shall not be seeing you soon."

"Please, Irvin, do not leave me or Charlotte. Let us converse. I will be better, and I will not be sick. I promise," Sybil begged.

"Your promises bear no truth anymore." And with that, Irvin left the room.

Sybil slumped in her chair, defeated and in despair. Was this how her marriage would be till her death? Would she receive no love from Irvin again? Would Charlotte not receive any love from her father? Did he plan to stay away forever?

But he is not her father, is he, Sybil? He was correct in his observation. It dawned on Sybil that he might know Charlotte was Hattie's child, but then, how could he? No one knew apart from a few people. Certainly, they would have not told anyone.

"My lady, oh dear Lord." Dollie rushed over as Sybil fell sideways to the carpet and vomited. The housekeeper was behind Dollie.

"Someone clear this up," she ordered. "We must get her to her chambers now."

"My lady, everything will be fine. Do not fret," Dollie crooned, taking Sybil by the arm and pulling her up gently. She wiped her mouth with a handkerchief.

"Oh, he has gone again, Dollie. Lord Fallow has left me again," Sybil cried. "I do not know what to do. Help me."

"She must rest, and she must see the doctor," Mrs. Wilks took charge. "Quickly, now."

※

Sybil lay on her bed, mumbling. Beads of perspiration lined her forehead as she tossed to and fro. Dollie wiped Sybil's forehead continuously.

"What has happened to my mother?" Charlotte rushed in. "Mama? What is happening?"

The doctor had arrived and attended to her, and now turned to Charlotte.

"Lady Fallow is resting as she should. However, I cannot understand the extent of her symptoms and distress," the doctor said. "I suggest perhaps a change in location, a trip to the coast would do her well. She will breathe in fresh sea air, which I have known to do extraordinary things to heal one's illnesses. A few weeks rest there, and she will be fine once more."

And so, Sybil's coastal retreat was arranged. As the carriage rolled away from the estate, Sybil stared outside with sad acceptance. She knew the real reason of her ill health, only she did not care to correct it anymore.

IT HAD BEEN Sybil's idea to purchase a house by the sea in the early months of her marriage. Irvin loved the sea as much as she did and had agreed to it immediately. As the carriage came into St. Ives, the sea air greeted her like a long-lost friend. Sybil breathed it in and enjoyed the smells of salt and seaweed. Seagulls circled above them, their cries shrill and urgent.

Charlotte and Dollie helped Sybil walk into the house in her frail state. Sybil smiled at them gratefully.

"Mama, you will certainly feel better here," said Charlotte. "I just know it."

Sybil placed a gentle hand on her cheek. "I feel it too... Charlotte, you must know that I love you very much."

"I know, Mama. I don't know what I would do without you. Do get better soon, I cannot see you in this state of illness much longer."

As the staff prepared the house, Sybil and Charlotte went to the beach. It was still quiet for it was morning. They sat on a blanket looking out to sea. Sybil placed her head on Charlotte's shoulder, feeling comfort and happiness, and perhaps even relief to leave the house where there was a husband and no love.

A ship passed by in the distance. It reminded her of the time she travelled with her own family from India to England when she was thirteen. Life had been good and well; both her parents loved one another, and she had loved them. Oh, how she missed her father now. He would have been very pleased to have Charlotte as his granddaughter, unlike her mother who had drifted away from her in recent years. It seemed Sybil's only happiness came from Charlotte.

That night, as Charlotte slept, Sybil and Dollie sat in the drawing room, which was warm with the fireplace burning. With Sybil not well, she felt the cold all too easily.

"Dollie, I am fearful. It is the reason why I am quite ill," said Sybil, as she stared into the fire.

"What are you fearing, my lady?" Dollie asked, concern on her face.

"A few days ago, when Lord Fallow and I had the same disagreement, he told me he did not believe Charlotte was his child. He said she looked nothing like us. Oh Dollie, do you believe he suspects she is Hattie's?"

"I don't think so. I am certain no one would have told him," said Dollie. "And you must believe that."

"I have a feeling that disturbs me," Sybil cried. "If Lord Fallow finds out the truth, that Charlotte is not his child… he may denounce us. We would have nowhere to go, and Charlotte will be ruined."

"Do not fret, my lady. We have kept this a secret from him for this long, surely, we can keep it from him for a long time more. He will not know."

"I do wish I had your faith, Dollie. There is something else. When I left the estate, I felt someone watching us. I turned to see who it is, but they were gone. I feel someone else knows our secret, and I will not be able to rest until I find out."

CHAPTER 9

DUNCAN, a man of thirty-one, stopped before the estate. The image of the lady with the red hair on the horse came to his mind. She was certainly different, like she didn't fit in with these people. And she seemed sad. The more Duncan thought about her, the more he thought she had a likeness to someone he knew, but he couldn't figure out who. Oh, how frustrating.

Placing a thin cigarette into his mouth, he looked through the bars of the black painted gates. Of course, he couldn't see the house, just a long road with tall trees and well-kept lawn on either side. How far was the house from the gates, and would he be able to get in without being noticed? Duncan always wanted to see how the toffs lived. He envied their wealth, which allowed them to do anything they wanted. And he disliked them. They thought too much of themselves, looking down on people like him—the poor, the town commoners who worked hard for their money.

There had been a man with the lady. He laughed at him, mocking him. Duncan's hand turned into a fist as fury rolled over him. He would get him, he would. How dare he laugh in his face. Duncan punched the wall, his eyes watering from the pain he received. He cursed out loud, and a couple passing stared at him, their eyebrows lifting.

"Git goin'!" he said, a growl under his throat. The man and woman walked away quickly.

***

"Did ya punch something, Dunc?" his brother, Michael asked as he walked into the house.

Michael, like the rest of Duncan's siblings, had all grown up and were adults. Michael was a good, strapping lad who worked at the shipyard and earned good money.

"No," Duncan grunted, lighting a cigarette. "'Do ya 'ave ya wages?"

"I' ave," said Michael, and grinned. "An I ain't givin' them t' ya." He took a chair and sat down, also lighting a cigarette. He blew some circles of smoke, which travelled to the ceiling. They dispersed, causing the smoke to unfurl like mist on water.

"You can' do that. I nee' the money, Mike," Duncan cried. "You can' cut me off, I owe them money. They'll kill me if I dun't pay 'em back, or the peelers will put me in debtor's jail. I must 'ave it!"

Duncan was desperate; he didn't want to go to jail or be the next victim story in the papers.

"If I 'adn't seen ya with that lot at the port, gamblin' away ma money, I wouldn't 've known. Why do ya do it? Come back to the shipyard, and you'll get your own money. Mum needs my wages for the house, an' she's sick. She need's ta see the doc."

"Mum's been ill for a long time. She's near 'er death bed, Mike. It doesn't mat'er, now."

Duncan felt the punch on his jaw before the pain, and he fell backward hitting the floor.

"You take tha' back, Dunc."

"What's 'appening 'ere?" Hattie arrived breathless with a bag of groceries. She looked in alarm from her eldest child to her middle child. "Michael, get off your brother!"

Duncan shrugged him off, though he was quite bigger than he was and much taller.

"It's nothin' Mum. I'm going out." Duncan seethed.

He roamed the streets in the dark of the night, worrying about where the money would come from now. He was sure Michael would have told his other brothers and sisters to not give him any, and so he had to find another way. And he was not going back to work at the shipyard.

When he returned home, Duncan found his mother awake. As like all the other times, she looked tired.

"Why aren't ya asleep?" he asked.

"I couldn't. I was worried about ya. Where do ya go at this time of night? And why did your brother hit ya?" Hattie shakily lit an oil lamp, illuminating the room.

"Never you mind. Mum ... I saw a lady today, she was young. I think she lives on da estate on the 'ill. Fair, she was with red hair like our Marigold and Katie. She looke' a lot like you. Isn't that strange?" Duncan stared at his mother's face, which paled. "Mum, are ya okay? Do ya know her?"

A memory of his mother... A child... She had died, or had she?

"What happened to Sally? Did she really die?" Duncan went over to Hattie and shook her shoulders. "Tell me!" He then sat down heavily next to her. The silence from his mother was the truth.

"I'm sorry, Dunc. I 'ad ta give 'her away. I needed da money, your pa just upped and left us when Sally was just a week old. What could I do?" Hattie began to cry.

"I wanna know who it was you gave her to. Tell me," Duncan demanded.

"I gave 'er to Lord and Lady Fallow. The lady you saw sounds like our Sally, but she is called Charlotte to the Fallows. I love 'er, Dunc, and I miss her very much. If I could have 'er back, I would. I think 'bout her every day, and I wanted 'er back with me, with us. Do ya believe me?"

He gaped at her. "You told us a lie, Mum. How could ya? She was our sista. Why dint ya tell me 'bout da money, that we couldn't afford Sally? I wudda worked 'arder for her. Yer told me she died when I was at work, an' I believe' ya."

Duncan tapped his foot; he had another sister. And she was rich, living comfortably in that big house with the toffs. She had the best dresses, the horses, and everyone to do her bidding. She didn't have to worry about earning to feed the family, and she was likely educated by a governess. He and his brothers and sisters had nothing; they had to scrape every penny to eat, to afford clothes, and to have a warm house.

Duncan wondered how much his mum got for Sally, probably a lot. He looked around the house they lived in and shook his head. So this was how they could afford to live here, because of the money from the Fallows. It all made sense; it was why they could leave the worst of the slums.

"Lord and Lady Fallow, did ya say?"

"Now, Dunc. I dun't want ya making any trouble, ya hear me? Sally is fine where she is now, she is 'appy and well. Dollie said so."

"Auntie Dollie knows?" Duncan couldn't believe it. But, of course, he remembered she worked as a lady's maid up there. "Who else knows?"

"Jus' Dollie, and now you."

Duncan stood up.

"Dunc, where ya goin' now?" Hattie was hysterical.

"I ain't goin' to da 'ouse. I'm just going' for a walk, but it ain't fair Sally gets to be rich and live in a big place. It ain't fair, Mum."

There has to be a way to make money out of this. If Sally can have it all, so can I.

He could even pay back the money he owed to those men, and escape going to jail. But he must come up with a plan, and then he would strike. This would work, he felt it in his bones.

He grinned, rubbing his hands in delight. He was going to be as rich as his little sister.

CHAPTER 10

Duncan pretended to be asleep, but kept an ear open, conscious of what was going on.

"I think 'e's asleep," whispered Marigold. Duncan knew they were talking about him.

"Good, now remember, we aren't to give 'im any more money. He'll waste it on gam'ling, 'e will." That was Michael.

"What if 'e aks fer it?" Marigold asked.

"Then, ignore him. You've 'idden it, right? Under the boards?"

"I did."

Ah, so the money was under the floorboards. When the house was finally empty, Duncan got up with glee. He looked at the floor, trying to figure out which board it was. They all looked like each other, loose and broken even. He couldn't lift them all up.

Duncan walked over each board, staring at them as if they would lift by themselves and reveal the money. Where would Margaret hide the money? It wouldn't be the ones under her bed, that would be too obvious. Maybe it was where the boys slept, but no, he didn't think it would be there. He thought hard; where would he not go? He didn't like going in the kitchen or the back yard. The back yard. There was a box there with boards inside. That was what Michael must have meant – under the boards.

Chuckling that he had found out their secret – how clever he was! – he went to the innocent looking box and opened the lid. There was a load of boards in there. One by one, he took them out, and after lifting the last one, there it was. The money. Duncan was careful to leave a few notes in there, now that he knew where the money was, he had free rein.

Over the next few weeks, Duncan watched the Fallows from behind the big house, coming and going in their expensive, private carriages. Every time he saw his sister, he was astounded at how she looked so much like their mother. There was no doubt she was Hattie's child. When he saw Dollie leave the servant's entrance, Duncan hid behind a large shrub. His blood boiled at seeing her because she was the one who had made all this happen. She was the one who took Sally away from them and allowed her this luxury.

He observed Charlotte and a woman leave the house most of the time; was that Lady Fallow? He never saw Lord Fallow though, which confused him. Where was he all this time? Maybe he was away on business, Duncan knew these landowners travelled a lot for business. If that was so, it could be to his advantage.

Hiding and following the women was not an easy thing, and money was running out fast. He needed money, and he'd made a plan on how to get it. He just needed to get Lady Fallow on her own.

※

"I come 'bout the job," Duncan told the butler. "The one about you needi' a groomsman?"

Duncan had been fortunate to hear about the opening in a tobacco shop one day. It was the perfect guise to talk to Lady Fallow when the time came.

"Do you know about horses, and how to groom them?"

"I do, sir," said Duncan. "I can drive too. I learned it."

"Do you have a reference? Where else have you worked?" the butler asked. He didn't seem to like Duncan, so Duncan had to make sure he did. And he knew someone who could forge a very good reference for him.

"I 'ave it with me, sir." Duncan produced a letter from his pocket and gave it eagerly to the butler. He didn't smile.

"All right, I will read it. And we will let you know if you have the job."

Duncan knew it was going to be hard to get that position, so he decided to speak to some people who would be able to twist the old butler's hand. He must get this job, or he wouldn't be able to carry out his plan.

That evening, Duncan sat with his friend around a tin fire. His friend was a known thief and a hoodlum. His friend would be very helpful to him.

"I need ya ta do somefin' fer me," Duncan spoke in a low voice, his eyes darting to see no one was near, no one was listening. The fire cackled in the silence.

"Yeah? What ya need doin'?"

"I wan' a job at the Fallow estate, see. An' the ol' butle' needs ta know 'ho's boss."

Duncan told him what the position was for, and that it was important.

"What's in it fer me?" his friend's marked face glowed red in the fire. He spat a twig out from his mouth, and put in a cigarette, lighting it with a flame.

"I'll give yer money from them people. I 'ave a plan, yer see.

Make sure no one else gets the job, and then the old butle' will 'ave no reason bu' ta give it to me."

THE ESTATE COACHMAN took Duncan around the stables, showing him his duties, and the horses.

"I don't think I've heard of you before," Mr. Harrison, the coachman, said. "Where did you say you've worked?"

"It was in Germany. I worked at a farm where they 'ad 'orses. You won't 'ave 'eard of it, though. I know how ta drive, too."

They stopped. "This is Lady Charlotte's horse. The horse is very special to her. It will be your duty to groom this horse and the others, too. Make sure the horse is always ready for Lady Charlotte."

Duncan stroked the horse's mane, and it backed away from him, neighing loudly.

Mr. Harrison laughed. "He doesn't like you, it seems. You'd better make him your friend and quick, too. He likes apples." The coachman took a red apple from his trouser pocket and tossed it to Duncan.

"Lady Charlotte wants to ride this afternoon. Have the horse cleaned right and groomed."

Duncan smiled. At last, he would be able to see his sister at close range, maybe even get to know her a little.

No, not yet. She mustn't get suspicious of me. I'm just the new groomsman.

Duncan had told his family he now had a job, but he lied about where it was. It wouldn't do any good to have his mother stop him if she knew the truth. And anyway, didn't she lie to him and his sisters and brothers about Charlotte? He was right; it was best to keep his secret for now.

"Lady Fallow is unwell, so Lady Charlotte won't be riding today," Mr. Harrison said to Duncan the next morning.

"What is the illness?" Duncan asked.

The coachman looked at Duncan, "Never you mind. That is the Fallow's business. You mind your work and see to all the horses. If I like your work in the next few weeks, I will let you manage more. And you might even get a rise in your pay."

"That's very good, Mr. Harrison. I won't disappoint ya."

And so, that was what he did. He didn't ask questions, and he just worked as hard as he could, sometimes doing extra jobs around the stables. Lady Charlotte's horse was always groomed first and kept happy. He was beginning to think her horse liked him now, for he wasn't aggressive with him anymore. The apples helped.

Mr. Harrison approved of Duncan's hard work and invited him to his quarters for dinner.

"It will be just me and me wife. She's a very good cook and generous too with her portions. And we'll talk about your pay, too."

Duncan arrived in his best clothes that evening. Maybe he could get some information about the Fallows when Mr. Harrison was mellow with the ale he brought. The cottage wasn't far from the house; it was necessary to be near the Fallows for they could want a driver at any time.

"Sit down, son," said Mr. Harrison, jovially. He showed him to a small round table.

The cottage was of a modest size, and well kept. The table was lit with a single oil lamp, and Duncan smelled the delicious dinner. Was it a roast? His stomach responded, and he laughed in embarrassment.

"I'm glad you are hungry." Mrs. Harrison came out of the kitchen with a pot, which she set down on the table. She went back to the kitchen and brought out the rest of the dinner.

They sat down to eat. Duncan was careful to not look so greedy and ate slowly.

"Mrs. Harrison, you cook well, you do. It's better than my mum's! But don't tell her I said tha'!"

"He's a lovely man, ain't he?" she said to her husband.

They finished eating, and Mrs. Harrison left the men sitting by the fire, drinking the ale. Mr. Harrison was most relaxed; it was a good time to ask him questions about the family.

"How long have ya worked fer da Fallows, Mr. Harrison?" Duncan asked, taking a long drink from his bottle. He was feeling mellow too, but he must stay alert. He wanted to know as much as possible about the family.

"I been here as long as I can remember. I started as a stable boy. And now I'm a coachman."

"What are they like?"

"Lord Fallow is a good employer, but we don't see him much here anymore. He is away on business a lot, you see. Lady Fallow is a kindly woman, but she is quiet and meek. She loves her daughter. I say, Lady Charlotte is a miracle child."

"Why do yer say tha'?"

"Well, Lady Fallow had three children before Lady Charlotte, and they all died. Poor woman, I would never want that to happen to my wife."

"I dunt see any children here," Duncan said.

"We don't have any, but we are happy enough," said Mr. Harrison. "Sometimes, Lady Charlotte comes here. Lady Fallow doesn't mind, but her father would. So, she comes when he is away."

"Lord Fallow sounds like a strict father," Duncan probed.

"Aye, he can be. One thing's for sure, I've never seen him talk to his daughter or ride with her. Lady Charlotte has always been with her mother. I do wonder if he loves her."

The coachman's eyes were becoming heavy. Duncan knew it was time to leave, after all, he had all the information he needed. He said his goodbye and left the man asleep in front of the fire.

THOUGHTS SWIRLED around Duncan's mind as he walked home, his hands in his pockets. It was a cool night, and he shuddered as a biting wind hit his shoulders. He'd have preferred to sleep in the stables if he were allowed. But it didn't matter, he kept warm by walking quickly to his house and thinking about the conversation he'd just had with the coachman.

He wondered if Lord Fallow knew about Charlotte's. Did he know she wasn't his daughter? Surely, he would've guessed as she looked nothing like him or his wife. Hmmm, it was something he'd have to find out.

And what about Lady Charlotte, didn't she think she was different from them? Couldn't she see the difference? Lady Fallow must have gone to some length to keep this secret quiet from society, surely. If it got out, it would be a right scandal.

And Lady Fallow would do anything to stop word from getting out, wouldn't she? She had so much to lose – her daughter, her husband, her home, and her status. Yes, she would do anything he asked her to.

CHAPTER 11

"How do you like your job?" Charlotte asked Duncan one fine morning as he saddled her horse with ease and accuracy.

"I like it very much, my lady," he said and helped her onto the horse, making sure she was comfortable.

"I spoke to Mr. Harrison, and he approves of your hard work. Therefore, I must congratulate you. The last groomsman was becoming slow, poor man, and had to retire. However, Mr. Harrison is happy now." She became aware the groomsman stared at her quite a lot, and it unnerved her.

She frowned. "Is there something you want to say? You continue staring at me, which is uninviting."

"My apologies, my lady. I didn't know I was doin' it. But if I may ask, why do you look so sad? Ain't it a beautiful day? Aren't ya 'appy you're going for a ride?"

"Is it so obvious?" She sighed.

"I have seen you many times as you come to ride your horse. Forgive me for observing you, but you remind me of ma sister, she's a lot like you, you see. She likes 'orses too and wants ta ride, but we are commoners. We can' afford 'em."

"If your sister wants to ride, why don't you bring her here one day? I will teach her," Charlotte said kindly. It would be an adventure to teach, and quite enjoyable.

"You are very kind, my lady. Katie won't believe it when I tell 'er... And my lady, you can trust me."

Charlotte considered telling the groomsman about her woes about her mother's illness, but it was not for a servant to know such intimate details of her family. This man was a new member of the staff household, and she could hardly trust him.

"It was nice talking to you." She clicked her tongue, and the horse trotted away.

To his surprise, Duncan found Charlotte to be lovely person. He wished he'd known her sooner, and if she hadn't been given away, they would have grown up as brother and sister. He would look after her as he used to do with his other siblings. But he couldn't let his emotions get in the way. He had a job to do, and that was get the money he needed.

It was his right, after what his mother, Auntie Dollie, and Lady Fallow did. He remembered what Mr. Harrison said about Lady Fallow's children being dead. Did he feel sorry for her? Maybe he did, but only a little bit. No, he had to remember why he was here, why he was going to blackmail the lady into giving him the money that would free him from those men and from the possibility of being thrown in prison.

DOLLIE PREPARED Sybil's clothes for the dinner she would be attending that evening. The party wasn't far, which was something to be thankful for. It was an invite from Lady Wordsworth, which extended to Lady Charlotte and Lord Fallow. It was no secret that Lord Fallow was away for most of the year, and gossip travelled among society that his relationship with his wife had fallen apart, and it was no secret that he was a recluse, bedding any woman coming his way.

She felt sorry for Lady Charlotte for not obtaining the love of a father, and she would sometimes observe her sitting alone, looking forlorn. Dollie sometimes even forgot who the girl really was, that she was, in truth, Hattie's child. Charlotte was remarkably like her real mother with her red hair and that smile. If Charlotte were to walk beside Hattie, there would be no mistake that they were mother and daughter.

Of course, she wouldn't tell this to Lady Fallow; it would certainly break her heart. It was already broken by her husband whom Dollie detested and wished gone. It hurt her to see her mistress cry every day, her health deteriorating. Why could the master not see it, that he was the cause of her melancholy? However, there was one special light that made Sybil happy, and that was Charlotte. God bless the child for she did everything she could to keep her mother in a joyful state of being.

Dollie hummed as she worked and was surprised to see Charlotte enter the room.

"Mama informed me you were here," she said, sitting on the bed.

"Does my lady require my attention?" Dollie asked.

"No. She is perfectly happy where she is. She is quite cheerful today, and I wonder if being at the sea did indeed make her feel better. Have you noticed she has colour back on her cheeks since returning? She doesn't seem as frail either."

Dollie smiled. "I understand you want to believe that, Lady Charlotte. But you have to see that she still requires healing, which is of the heart. Only then will she become better – in her body and in her mind."

"What else can we do, Dollie?" Charlotte asked. She took Dollie's hand. "We took her to the coast, and the doctor has been to see her. Is there anything else we could try?"

Dollie could not tell her the truth that was worrying Sybil, the one that could ruin her and Charlotte, the one that could destroy their lives if Lord Fallow found out. How could she tell this child that her mother was not her mother, and if the truth came out... Ach, the outcome did not bear thinking about.

"Did you have a nice ride today?" Dollie asked.

"Indeed," said Charlotte. "I feel free when I ride. I went to the river and chose to dip my feet into the water. There is something charming about nature, do you not believe? Perhaps I may take Mama there. It will heal her soul as it does mine."

Charlotte walked to the window and looked out.

"I spoke to the new groomsman today, Dollie. He looks awfully familiar. I feel like I know him. I do not understand why that is."

"I was not aware we recruited someone new. What is he like?"

"He is younger than the last one. Mr. Harrison told me his name is Duncan and he lives not far from here. He is a nice man, and he talks a lot, unlike the old groomsman. He told me his sister, Katie, likes to ride. I have invited him to bring her to the estate one day."

The colour on Dollie's face drained away.

"Was that wrong of me?" Charlotte asked.

"You are a kind person. You... You did nothing wrong. Can you describe him to me?" Dollie hoped it wasn't who she thought it was. There could be other brothers and sisters with the same names, surely.

"Well, he has green eyes and dark hair. He is also quite tall."

Dollie forced a smile on her face. "Well, isn't that lovely? Now, Lady Charlotte, should you not be getting along to your next lesson? Miss Granger will be waiting for you."

As soon as Charlotte was away, with a rapidly beating heart, Dollie sat down. It couldn't be him; certainly, Hattie would have told her. Unless she didn't know her son had taken a job at the estate. If it was him, then he has seen Charlotte. Would he be clever enough to realise she looked like his mother? Or did he know Charlotte was indeed the child of Hattie Kennedy? Well, there was one way to find out.

Dollie looked into the drawing room where Sybil was resting with a blanket over her. A book lay on her chest. Dollie removed it gently and placed it on the small table to her right and adjusted the cover. And then she tiptoed away. The short walk to the stables seemed like a long time to reach, but when she did, Dollie was careful to not be seen by this man.

If it was him, she didn't want to speak to him. Not until she knew what was going on. She wanted to know if this was the

Duncan she knew and why he chose to get a job here. Dollie crept to the side of the stables where she knew the groomsmen worked and peeked around the corner. He had his back turned to her, so she was unable to see his face.

"Oh!" she grumbled.

The man turned, and it was confirmed. It was, indeed, Duncan. She wanted to go to him, demand answers, shake him if it had to be. But she couldn't. Not yet. Sybil had said she felt someone was watching her when she came and left the estate. Could it have been Duncan all along? Was he spying on the family? What did he want, and why was he doing this?

Be patient, Dollie. All would surely be revealed soon.

So, for now, Dollie made sure Lady Fallow and Lady Charlotte did not leave the house without a chaperone, or herself. Lady Charlotte was not to go riding – she would have to get her away from the house. But how that was going to be possible, Dollie had no idea.

CHAPTER 12

"My lady, I believe you and Lady Charlotte should not travel alone." Dollie curled a strand of Sybil's hair in the iron tongs. "It is not safe."

Sybil turned to look at Dollie in the mirror. "Why do you say that?" There was worry in her tone.

"You have told me you feel there is someone following you, and I am uneasy who that could be." Sybil let down a strand from the tongs, and it curled beautifully. Dollie took another strand of hair. "With Lord Fallow away most of the time, the estate is vulnerable to undesired visits from other men, and also possibly assaults. I would be content if you took someone with you when you go out on an excursion, and I believe Lady Charlotte should not ride for a little while alone. If she persists, perhaps she could ride with someone she is acquainted with... And I have one last thought, it would be better if she did not talk to the new groomsman."

"Is there something about him I should be concerned about?" asked Sybil. "As you are aware, I do not mind Charlotte conversing with the servants."

"I agree it is a lovely to do so, but even with the working class we know, we must not exceed our status. Becoming too familiar with the servants does not fare well."

Dollie wondered if she should tell Sybil about Duncan, who he was. But then decided against it. The truth would only make her mistress more anxious, and her health would deteriorate further.

"It is nothing more, my lady. I just don't trust the groomsman, and neither should Lady Charlotte. I know the man, you see, and while he is a good person and a hard worker, you can never know what may happen when a servant and a naïve child become close." Dollie knew this would not happen. Duncan had come here on another motive, she was sure. She wondered if he knew Charlotte was his sister. "Do you agree with me, my lady?"

"Oh dear," said Sybil. "Do you think something could happen? Charlotte may be young; however, she understands the rules."

"I have seen this before. A servant and a Lady begin by becoming familiar, which leads them to court in secrecy. And then they elope without consent. It is likely this could happen. If you agree, I would like to accompany you on all journeys, my lady." Dollie was aware she was frightening her mistress. "Do not fret. I am only being cautious."

"Certainly, Dollie, if you believe it is necessary," Sybil said hesitantly. "You know the working class better than I, and I trust your character. Very well, then."

Dollie, now satisfied that Sybil and Charlotte would be protected from Duncan, could breathe more freely.

Sunlight flooded the drawing room, brightening every dark corner. Sybil had the windows opened, wanting to feel the warm air. Oh, how pleasant it felt on her skin. Melodious music flowed from Charlotte's practiced fingers on the pianoforte, and Sybil hummed along.

"I must agree that your skill for playing the pianoforte is becoming delightful, my dear," Sybil praised her.

"Oh, do you believe it so, Mama? I am so pleased you do. And I have been practicing every day." Charlotte stopped playing and turned toward her mother, placing her hands on her lap. "I wish Papa was here to see me."

Sybil smiled as brightly as she could, trying to ignore the feeling of sadness for her child. "Papa would like it very much."

"I know you're not telling the truth, Mama. Papa is hardly here anymore…" Charlotte left her piano seat and went to sit by her mother. Sybil took her hand in hers, comforted by her daughter's love.

Sybil could see that Charlotte was very different to her and Irvin. Perhaps it was obvious she was not like either of them. To Sybil, Charlotte was her daughter, and no one could take that away from her. Her momentary happiness vanished as the image of Irvin's temper came to her mind. He pointed to her, his face twisted.

"I know she was not our child! Whose is she? Do you have a lover?" That was how Irvin would accuse her. He would disown her and Charlotte. Oh, what would they do if it happened?

"Mama? Are you all right?" asked Charlotte. "Are you feeling ill again?"

"No, my dear, I am fine."

"I say we go for an excursion to the park. It is a lovely day, and you would enjoy it thoroughly," Charlotte said. "Will we go?"

Sybil thought about Dollie who had gone to the village. She would not be back for hours.

"I believe we should travel with a trusted person, Charlotte. Dollie is not here, perhaps we should wait for her to return?"

"Why Mama? We usually travel together, we do not need to waste Dollie's time, surely?"

"I only remembered that Mr. Harrison is quite ill. He will not be able to drive us," Sybil said, hoping Charlotte would drop the suggestion of the excursion, or wait until Dollie returned.

"I have a solution. We can ask the new groomsman, Mama. He told me during a conversation that he has learned to drive a carriage. How wonderful, is it not? I will ask for him to take us in an hour."

"I was not aware you spoke freely with the groomsman," commented Sybil.

"Is that a problem?" Charlotte asked softly, melting Sybil's heart.

"No, my dear. But you must be careful with the servants you speak to. We cannot trust anyone to not converse about the family and spread things around the village. Your father's disappearance from the house and what he does is already a scandal. I do not want anything further. But for now, we will go to the park."

Sybil smiled, but she was indeed frightened. She hoped Dollie would come back soon.

"MY LADY," Duncan said as Sybil and Charlotte came to the carriage.

"How long have you been driving?" asked Sybil carefully. She could not trust this man, not after what Dollie told her.

"For many years, my lady," Duncan replied, giving her a big smile. "I will be careful, my lady. Do not worry."

"I am used to Mr. Harrison driving us," said Sybil. "But very well. Take us to Hyde Park."

Charlotte smiled at Sybil, squeezing her arm. They sat in their seat, enjoying the warm air blowing from the open window as the carriage rolled toward the park. But Sybil couldn't relax as there hovered the feeling of mistrust in her mind. She should have heeded Dollie's warning. The groomsman seemed friendly and confident enough, and she wanted to believe he was a good man, but still...

When she had looked closely at him earlier, she was bewildered to notice he resembled Charlotte in some ways. The freckles, and the eyes indeed were very alike. And his smile, too.

No, I am thinking too much. He is nothing like my Charlotte. My mind is playing games, certainly. How silly I am.

"Mama, I received an invite today from Lady Anne. She has invited me to a party and would like me to stay with her for a week," said Charlotte.

"What a splendid invitation. Have you accepted?"

"I would not without your permission, Mama. I may decline, for you are still quite ill. Who will look after you when I am gone? Papa is not here."

"My dear Charlotte, you are most kind to me, and I am very grateful. But my love, I cannot deny you such happiness. I insist you accept immediately when we return home. I will not be alone, as you well know. I have Dollie and the household staff. So, you see, you have no excuse."

"If you insist, I shall accept."

The afternoon became very pleasant as the ladies promenaded in the park. They had an ice each, and then boated. Sybil looked up at the light blue sky and the hazy sun, forgetting her woes for a while. Around them, couples and young families laughed as the men rowed the boats. The children squealed when the boats rocked from side to side, often with a nanny holding tightly onto them. Sybil remembered when she would take Charlotte out like this, yet they were always alone. Irvin never accompanied them, which was indeed a pity.

CHAPTER 13

As the carriage arrived back to the estate, Sybil began to feel uneasy. The contentment she had experienced at the park now diminished, and her anxiety began to show once more. Still, Sybil pretended everything was all right for Charlotte's sake. The weather seemed to respond to her darkening feelings, as thick clouds gathered blocking the sun.

"I do not like this," she murmured. "They are foreboding."

"They are only clouds, Mama. You must not read into it too much," Charlotte said gently. "You are aware how weather can change rapidly. Do not alarm yourself."

Of course, Charlotte was right. She was becoming frantic unnecessarily. But Dollie's voice spoke in her head again. *Do not trust*. Sybil shivered as if cold water slid down her spine.

At last, they arrived home. Charlotte disembarked first, then helped Sybil down.

"My lady, can I have a moment to talk with yer?" Duncan asked. "It' private, and I want to speak to you alone."

Surprised, Sybil looked from Charlotte to the groomsman.

"I will leave you two, then," said Charlotte.

"No, do not leave," said Sybil, her mouth becoming dry, and her heartbeat becoming rapid. "Whatever you have to say can be said with Lady Charlotte present."

"Mama, it is fine. I do not mind. I will be in the library." And then to her horror, Charlotte left them.

"Please come this way, my lady," Duncan said amicably.

Sybil followed, though she did not like this at all. They went to the side of the house where no one was likely to venture. It was very dark here, making Sybil more nervous.

Duncan turned to her. His smile dropped, and his eyes narrowed.

"Now, listen to me, Lady Fallow. I know yer secret, the one you been keeping all this time."

"Secret? There is no secret."

"You know what I'm on about. You should stop pretendin'," Duncan spoke. "I know who Lady Charlotte is. I know she ain't yers." His tone was deadly calm.

"Charlotte is my child." Sybil tried to speak strongly, but even she could hear the shaking in her voice. "And it is not your place to question your employer."

She detested herself for it; she *was* Charlotte's mother, and she should be able to declare it with ease and confidence. But her voice was halting, unsure.

He simply stared at her.

"Who ... told you?" she finally uttered.

Duncan's laugh put more fear into her. "That's none of yer business, my lady. Now, listen. If yer want me to keep it quiet, you'll 'ave to give me some money."

"I d-don't have any money," Sybil said, her stomach churning.

"Yer lying. You, the lady of the house, don't 'ave yer own money? I don't believe it. I want five pounds to start. You get me the money, an' I'll keep quiet. Do yer understand? I'll wait till Saturday. If I dunt 'ave it by then, your sweet daughter will know about her birth. That's a promise."

DOLLIE WALKED up the path of the estate, hoping the threatening rains wouldn't come. A wind had picked up, and she felt something ominous in the air. She walked faster now, wishing she had stayed at the house. She feared for Sybil, had something happened to her? Was she in distress? Above her, lightning flashed and seconds later, she heard the rumble of thunder. Her legs began to move faster, and then she began to run as it rained.

Out of breath, she rushed into the house. She took a minute to collect herself.

"Dollie, are you all right?" asked the housekeeper. "Where have you been?"

"To the village shops," said Dollie. "I was caught in the rain, unfortunately." She paused, and then asked, "Can you tell me where Lady Fallow is? I fear I left her for too long."

"She's been asking for you, too. You will find her in her bedchamber."

Dollie thanked the housekeeper, and soon she was standing outside Sybil's door. She knocked softly and went inside. A fire burned cheerily, illuminating Sybil's frightened expression as she sat on a chair beside it. She was engrossed in the flames and the warmth; Dollie didn't want to alert her of her presence. Sybil's demeanour alarmed her. What had happened in her absence?

"My lady…" she said gently.

Sybil turned to her, her eyes wide with fright. "I have done something … silly, Dollie. It is all my fault. I should have listened to you and stayed home. Oh, what do I do now?" she cried. She rocked to and fro, her arms wrapped around herself.

"What happened? Do tell me immediately." Dollie sat with her.

"I... I went to Hyde Park with Charlotte," Sybil said.

"Who accompanied you?" Dollie asked, fearing the worst. Sybil confirmed it by shaking her head.

"Mr. Harrison was ill, so the groomsman drove us."

Dollie didn't know Duncan could drive.

"And when we reached home, he ... he threatened me. He knows about Charlotte—he knows she is not my daughter."

"Did he say he knows whose daughter she is?" Dollie asked quickly.

"He did not. But he wants five pounds to keep his silence. How do I obtain that money? Lord Fallow is not here. Besides, if he were, he hardly converses with me, and he would not let me have it. I am ruined, Dollie. And it is my fault. Why did I not listen to you?"

Dollie didn't know how to console her mistress, but she couldn't stand to see her so miserable.

"My lady. It is no fault of yours certainly. I have a confession, and I am sorry to have to tell you this. I knew who the groomsman was when I asked you to stop Lady Charlotte from talking to the man. He is the son of Hattie, Charlotte's real mother. And now I know she's told him the truth about her. That's why the groomsman is blackmailing you."

There was silence from Sybil, and Dollie wondered if she was going to tell her to leave the household, and that she would no longer be needed to work as her lady's maid. It was certainly a miserable thought. Dollie loved Lady Fallow and Lady Charlotte. She loved her position and could not think to work at any other house.

"I understand if you are angry with me and want me to leave employment..." Dollie said.

Sybil looked at her as if she had gone mad. She laughed.

"Oh, Dollie. Is that what you believe? Why would I want to relieve you of your duties when you are the one person who keeps me sane and looks after me? You have been with me for so long. You have seen my three failures to bring a child into this world, and you are my confidante. I trust you more than I trust anyone else, apart from Charlotte, of course. But she is only a child, and she does not yet know the truth.

"I do not require you to leave me and the house. There is one thing you can do for me, something which may keep the groomsman happy for a while. There are two candlesticks that are very expensive. They would fetch the five pounds we need to pay him. Tomorrow, I wish you to go to into town and sell them for five pounds."

"If we pay him now, he will come back for more. Duncan Kennedy is proving to be a very greedy man. I have a mind to speak to his mother and see if she can stop this behaviour."

"No, do not do that. We cannot burden her, too. Oh, Dollie, if Charlotte finds out about her real parentage... I cannot bear to think about it. Take the candlesticks tomorrow and bring back the money. I want it paid to the groomsman immediately."

Dollie would do as her mistress wished, although she believed it to be a very bad decision.

CHAPTER 14

DOLLIE PASSED the two candlesticks to the man who eyed her suspiciously.

"How can I be certain these were not stolen from the house where you work? You are what, a maid, am I correct? You have come to sell these for your own gain," the man declared, peering over his glasses.

"Sir, I am no thief, and I would not dream of stealing. My mistress has given me a letter of permission to sell the candlesticks. She does not want this repeated, mind. I hope to have your cooperation." Dollie took the letter from her bag and passed it into the man's hand. He adjusted his glasses and read it.

"It all seems fair and true," he grunted, not seeming to want to admit he was wrong. Dollie managed to keep her smile inside.

"Lady Fallow requires five pounds, and no less. Those are her instructions."

"Very well," the man said.

He didn't try to haggle, and she wondered if the candlesticks were worth much more. However, Lady Fallow wanted only five so Dollie decided not to ask for more.

Taking the money, she went straight to see Duncan at the stables. Thankfully, he was alone.

"What do yer want?" he asked, quite unkindly, upon her approach. "Shouldn't yer be attending to yer precious mistress?" Dollie was unaccustomed to this Duncan, who had always been polite to her.

"Why are you here, Duncan? Why are you working on this estate?" were her first questions.

Duncan continued to brush the flank of the horse he was attending to, ignoring Dollie's question. Dollie waited.

"What do you know about Lady Charlotte?"

Duncan's face broke into a malicious smile, which made her flinch.

"I know 'ho she is, Auntie Dollie. She is ma sister, ain't she?

And you made me mum give 'er away." Duncan didn't shout. He said it in a calm voice which executed a confidence.

He stopped attending to the horse and turned to face her.

"I was angry when Mum admitted da truth to me. When I first saw Charlotte 'ere, she looke' so familiar, so much like our Katie and Mum, too. Mum said Charlotte was our Sally, that you came to the house that day to find a child."

"What else did Hattie tell you?"

Did Hattie tell him about the children Lady Fallow had lost?

"Nothin' else." Duncan shrugged. "All I know is tha' Charlotte is ma sister. An' tha' you took her ta give to the Lady. But why did ya do it, Auntie Dollie? Why take me sister?"

"Your mother was finding it hard to feed another child, Duncan. And we were paying her handsomely. It is why you live in a good house. Please understand and leave Lady Fallow and Lady Charlotte alone," pleaded Dollie.

"But Charlotte ain't no real lady, is she? She is a commoner like we are, an' she should know 'ho 'er real mum is. 'nd I will tell, I will tell her if need be. Don't think I won't. Why does she ge' a betta life than me an' my brothers 'nd sisters? I want da money, tell that to your mistress."

"I have the money." Dollie took it out of her bag and handed him the wad of currency. "Now you must promise me something. You can't ask for anymore. You have enough."

Dollie made to walk away but then stopped.

"I am disappointed in you, Duncan. I never thought you would become so evil and selfish." She was shaking as she finally walked away.

CHARLOTTE WATCHED the exchange between Dollie and Duncan from afar, unable to catch what they were talking about. It was clearly not a pleasant conversation, and she thought she heard some exclamations on Dollie's part, although she couldn't be certain. She wondered if Dollie knew him well before, after all, they were the same class. No, no. Why should Dollie know him because they were both working class? She felt ridiculous for thinking it. But then, he was Hattie's son...

CHARLOTTE WALKED BACK to the house only to find a carriage outside. She was confused; they were not expecting any visitors. Someone cleared his throat, and she turned round to see Dwight.

"Oh, Dwight... I mean Mr. Calverton." She curtseyed, making him laugh.

"Lady Charlotte," he bowed.

They both laughed.

"Let us go inside," Charlotte said. "Why did you not write you were coming? When did you arrive from Germany?"

They entered the house and proceeded straight to the drawing room.

"Do alert Mama of Mr. Calverton's arrival," she told the butler. "Now, Dwight, you must answer my questions. I am eager to learn it all."

"First, I did not write to alert you of my visit for I wanted to surprise you. Second, I am on a short break from the firm. My generous employer agreed on my leave. After meeting with Papa, I came straight here to see you."

"And why did you want to see me?" A coy smile played on Charlotte's face.

"I must say I missed you," he said. He stood with his arms behind his back, straight and very handsome. He had longer hair now, and he looked older, too. When Dwight looked into her eyes, she found her face growing warm.

"Charlotte, I would like to spend the days I am here with you, if you would allow. My days in Germany have been empty without you, and I cannot bear to be away for long periods of time."

Charlotte was taken aback by this, surprised at his words.

Dwight closed the gap between them, and took her hand in his, which was very bold.

"I can think of no one else," he said.

The door opened, and Dwight stepped away quickly.

"Mr. Calverton, how lovely to have you here," Sybil said.

To Charlotte's relief, she did not seem to have noticed Dwight's adventurous declaration, or that he held her hand, which he now quickly dropped.

"Lady Fallow." He bowed.

"Did you come alone?" Sybil enquired.

"I did. Papa could not come away, and Mama is busy with her committees. I hope you do not mind me arriving unannounced?"

"Certainly not. You are very welcome here." Sybil looked at Charlotte then back at him. "Lord Fallow is not here, I am afraid. You will have to amuse yourself with me and Charlotte, if you do not mind so much."

"Not at all, Lady Fallow."

"Well, I will leave you two to converse," said Sybil. "I have some correspondence to attend to."

Charlotte was both surprised and grateful that her mother did not mind leaving her alone with Dwight, unchaperoned. It was unusual, indeed.

PART III

CHAPTER 15

HATTIE WATCHED Duncan lying on the bed, his eyes closed. She was worried about him, and that was the truth. Every so often he brought money home. He said he found work, and his boss paid him generously for his hard work. But she wasn't convinced he was telling the truth. No one paid anyone that kind of money unless one worked in high places. Duncan had no such skill or education. He was lying to her.

She coughed and pain travelled through her body. She knew she was fading, losing her grip on this world. But how could she tell her children? Having a doctor see her was not a solution, for how would they be able to afford it?

"Duncan, tell me, where' are ya gettin' the money from? Tell me da truth." Her tone was quiet, but it sounded deafening in the house. It was only she and Duncan.

Duncan sat up on his bed.

"I told ya, I get paid by ma boss." His tone was rough. "Why'dya keep on askin'?"

"It ain't natural to get so much money. I dunt wanna see ya in prison, Dunc. It's not illegal, is it?"

"Nah, it ain't. It's 'onest work, it is."

"All right, if you say so," Hattie said.

"Why dunt you believe me? If it were Michael or the others, you would believe 'em, wouldn' ya?" Duncan's eyes blazed with anger, and it scared her.

"They 'ave good jobs. They dunt sneak around in the night or come back with lots a money."

"Well, I dunt care what ya think, Mum."

"You used ta be my good boy, what 'appened to ya?" Hattie sighed. She coughed, and this time she saw blood on her sleeve.

"I grew up, Mum. An' if y hadn't lied to me in the first place, I might not… "

"What Dunc? What wudda you might not 'ave done?"

"Nuthin'. I'm going out."

As Duncan went by his mother, aiming for the door, Hattie

took hold of his shirt and stopped him. She stood up, and went to stand by the door, blocking him with her frail body.

"Get outta the way, Mum."

"No. I won't. Stay 'ere with me." Hattie decided to tell him the truth. "Look Dunc, I'm dying."

"Then I'll get the doctor," he said, clearly thinking she was exaggerating.

"It's too late," Hattie sighed. "I jus' need ya with me. I dunt wanna die alone."

Hattie began to cough violently, her body shaking. She then collapsed.

"Mum!" Duncan cried. He picked her up and took her to the bed, laying her down. "I'll get some water."

When Duncan flicked some water on to his mother, she opened her eyes. She raised her frail hand and placed it on his cheek.

"What's 'appened to Mum?" Marigold asked, standing by the door. "Why's she on the bed? Dunc, what's happened?" She came in with the other siblings following. "She is so pale."

"Mum. Mum?" Katie cried.

Albert, Edith, and Michael all gathered around their mother. Hattie's face had gone a strange dull colour. Her eyes were foggy, but she tried to smile. The result made all the children go deathly quiet.

"I love ... ya all, my children," she said, her voice faltering. "Tell Sally, I love her too, won't ya, Dunc?"

"Mum, 'ho's Sally?" asked Michael.

Hattie let out a sigh, closing her eyes. She was gone.

THREE MONTHS LATER.

Duncan knelt before his mother's grave. It was a pauper's grave, unmarked with a fancy tombstone. With him was Michael. After they paid their respects, they stood.

"I gotta go," Duncan said.

"Not yet. I want some answers. Who's Sally, Dunc?" Michael was persistent. "Why did Mum say she loved 'er?"

"She's no one. I told ya all," Duncan grunted. "Mum told me she worked in a workhouse, that's all." He could lie expertly, and he was right glad of it.

"You're lying," Michael said.

"I ain't. Leave it, Mike," Duncan said, annoyed.

"I won't," Michael cried. "And I'm sick of the way you act. You treat us all like scum."

Duncan's temper surged, and he went at his brother, knocking him to the ground.

Michael fell to the dirt, his nose a bloody mess. He got up immediately and charged at Duncan. They rolled around on the muddy ground, punching and kicking each other, oblivious to the shouts from onlookers.

"Oi! What's going on 'ere?" a peeler shouted, pulling them apart.

Duncan and Michael gave each other murderous stares.

"You two brothers?" the peeler asked looking from one to the other.

"Yes," said Michael and spat.

"Well, I'll let ya off this time, but I dunt wanna see ya two again. Now, get on."

"Yes, sir," said Duncan and Michael together.

※

DUNCAN KICKED a glass bottle and watched it roll. The night was too dark, and it only made him angrier. He would have paid for a proper grave for his mother if only he'd had the money for it. But it was running out again and quicker than before.

He would have to speak to Lady Fallow again. He still didn't tell his sisters and brothers the truth. If they found out who Sally was, and how he was blackmailing her new family, the money would stop coming in. And he would be in more trouble than before.

Since the funeral, Duncan hadn't spoken with his brothers and sisters, apart from Michael, who chose to keep an eye on him. The others were often out, making their way somehow with their own jobs—he didn't know how, and he didn't care. Duncan had no doubt that they still spoke with each other, just not to him.

He didn't care. He had his own problems to deal with. Duncan drank deeply of his ale, feeling the brown potent drink run down his throat. It made it all the better. Dogs barked in the distance and some fool sang at the top of his voice. Duncan headed back home, the one place where he still felt safe even if his family would already be asleep and would likely not even know he was there. He felt his mum was still looking out for him, even though he had gone down a bad route, and there was no way out of it.

His eyes felt heavy as he opened the door of the house, and he fell straight onto the floor, where he laid until morning.

"I WANT MORE MONEY," Duncan demanded, standing by the side of the house.

"I cannot give you anymore," Sybil said. "I have nothing left in the house to sell without it being noticed. Besides, you have had some money every month. Is that not enough?"

Sybil wrung her hands, looking around her nervously.

"Look, I'm in debt. If I dunt pay those men, I'll be in jail. And if I go ta jail, I'll sing loud and long. I'll tell everyone what you did fifteen years ago."

Sybil's face went pale, almost translucent. She licked her dry lips. "No, please do not do that. I will lose everything, and I do not want to hurt Charlotte."

Duncan laughed, "She'll find out soon 'nuff. She's a clever kid."

"Then let it be a secret for a little longer, I beg you. I will find the money, and you can have it one last time. Just do not ask again."

"I ain't promisin' tha'. All right, I'll give ya seven days."

At the sound of a carriage arriving, Duncan hid further in the shadows but didn't leave. Sybil hurried away, casting one look behind her.

"Lady Calverton, Mr. Calverton," she greeted them.

"What are you doing out here, Lady Fallow?" asked Lady Calverton, surprised. "Were you alone?" She tried to look behind Sybil, and then frowned, seeming to find no one there.

"I went for a promenade. I only just came back," Sybil explained, hoping mother and son would believe her unlikely story. She smiled as brightly as she could, although the meeting with Duncan had unnerved her again. "Let's proceed inside, shall we?"

"Allow me accompany you, Lady Fallow," Dwight said kindly. He jumped down and took Sybil's gloved hand in his and led her inside. His eyes seemed to be searching for someone.

"Are you looking for Charlotte?" she asked.

"I was wondering if she was in the house," Dwight said, sheepishly "But no matter if she is otherwise engaged."

"My dear, she is in the library. Dollie, would you show Mr. Calverton there, and then ask for some tea to be brought into the drawing room."

"Certainly, my lady."

As Dollie led him away, she and Lady Calverton made themselves comfortable in the drawing room.

"You look rather ill," Lady Calverton observed. "Should you be up at all? I would think you would be better confined to your bedchambers. Is there something you are particularly concerned about?"

"It is just ... some household troubles. However, I am perfectly well now. I prefer to be kept busy, as the day can begin to become dire and tedious, do you not believe so?"

Sybil asked. She avoided looking at her visitor's face directly. "It was unfortunate we missed you last time Lord Calverton paid a visit. He informed us you had a cold."

"It was a minor ailment, nothing to be concerned about." Lady Calverton seemed to be a little irate about her illness, so Sybil decided to take the conversation elsewhere.

"I hear there is a new art gallery opening. There is quite a fuss about it. Do you intend to visit?"

"No, I do not. I do not care so much for art."

"Is it not lovely to see Mr. Calverton and Charlotte becoming quite acquainted again, after a long absence. Lady Calverton, I was hoping to discuss something which you may find delightful."

"What is that?"

"Charlotte will be of age soon. It has come to my attention that she and Mr. Calverton have been spending a lot of time together when he is in England, and I suspect they are becoming close. I would like to put forward the proposal of a marriage between them when the time arrives." Sybil held her breath, hoping for a good reaction.

"My dear, I would think that would come from her father and not from you. Dwight's attention needs to be directed toward his work, not women and not your daughter. He will have time for that later. I find her distracting for Dwight, and perhaps a little childish in her mannerisms. She does not seem quite ready to come out yet."

Lady Calverton straightened her gloves and her cap.

"Besides, you mentioned you had difficulties in your household which I can assume is financial, considering the gossip," she continued. "This does not bode well since we would want a handsome dowry. Where would you get it from? Not from your husband who is spending all his wealth on other ... um, pursuits." Lady Calverton's sharp tone made Sybil gasp.

"Do not pretend you are unaware, Lady Fallow. So, do excuse me if we are reluctant to give our approval and permission for Dwight to marry your daughter. I would prefer him to find a woman who is quite stable and who does not have a fragmented family."

Sybil blinked back tears. She felt as if she had been slapped. But Lady Calverton was correct, where would she obtain a worthy dowry? She had sold all her jewellery and some old keepsake items, as well as vases and silverware to pay the groomsman. She was quite destitute.

Sybil also did not know if there was any money left in her husband's accounts, and she could not ask Irvin. She had doubts whether he would even allow a marriage between Dwight and Charlotte. Oh, what a dilemma this was.

CHAPTER 16

CHARLOTTE WATCHED SLANTED raindrops splash on her window. The sky was a combination of night blue and mauve. Lightning illuminated the dark room, and thunder rumbled above them moments later. A maid added more coal to the fireplace, and the flames danced on her pretty face. She looked young, perhaps sixteen. Charlotte couldn't be certain. Involuntarily, she shivered as if darkness was upon them, and her thoughts led her to her mother.

She couldn't understand why her mother was becoming paler by the day, she should be gaining colour back in her cheeks and gaining strength. Something was troubling her and Charlotte intended to find out what it was.

Suddenly she jumped as a loud crack sounded above them. The maid looked up in alarm.

"That frightened me, it did," the maid said.

"You may go now," Charlotte said. "There is no more to do here. And perhaps have some sweet tea to soothe your nerves.

When she was alone, Charlotte remembered something from when she was probably not more than nine years old. It was a day like this, and Sybil cradled her to her bosom singing a sweet soothing song. It had calmed her frightened heart. But now, her mother was lying in bed beside where Charlotte sat. She mumbled something incoherent. She tossed, her hands clammy from the fever.

"Oh, Mama. Please get better. I cannot bear to see you like this," she whispered, tears falling down her cheeks. Charlotte stroked her forehead as a mother would do for her child and kissed it gently. She took one of Sybil's hands, and it was so thin.

"I will call Dollie and Mrs. Wilks, Mama. I believe you need to see the doctor, too."

Dollie was the first to arrive, with Mrs. Wilks following close behind.

"Is Her Ladyship no better?" asked Dollie, checking Sybil over. "Dear Lord, she is burning. When did the fever start?"

"I do not know, perhaps an hour ago," Charlotte said, her voice faltering. "I do not know what to do. We must call the doctor straight away."

"Hush now, child," Mrs. Wilks led Charlotte away. "Dollie will sit with your mother, and we will fetch the doctor. It was right you summoned us."

The housekeeper and Charlotte went downstairs and met with the butler.

"We must call for the doctor immediately for Lady Fallow," she said. "She has a fever."

"Very well. I will go with the carriage driver," the butler said.

"All right," said Mrs. Wilks. "That is a fine idea."

"I want to go, too," said Charlotte. "Do not deny me that, please. I feel I must do something."

"No, Lady Charlotte, we cannot let you do that. The weather is most treacherous, and you must be safe with us here," the butler advised.

"All right, but do hurry," Charlotte said.

CHARLOTTE PACED the corridor of the mezzanine floor. The rains continued relentlessly; the sky turned darker yet. She couldn't take it any longer and flew down the steps to the front door. Rain and wind battered her as she opened the door, but she didn't care. She waited to see a light or hear the carriage drawing near.

"What are you doing, Lady Charlotte? Come away at once, and let's have you dressed in something dry. You are completely wet." Dollie tried to pull Charlotte away, but she stayed, standing firm.

"I do not care if I am wet. I will not leave until they arrive with the doctor."

"Oh, you are stubborn," said Dollie, shaking her head. Just then, a set of swingling oil lamps came into view, and she let out a sigh as did Charlotte. They both rushed down the steps.

"Lady Charlotte!" the doctor exclaimed, taking in her drenched clothes, then looking at Dollie.

"Come, quick," Charlotte took the old doctor's arm and hurried him along. "Mama needs attention immediately."

"Mr. Donaldson has filled me in," the doctor said. "Now, you get changed out of your wet clothes. I do not want to be treating another lady of the house with a fever! You, too, Dollie."

A few minutes later, Charlotte was changed into another dress and standing in a corner of the room as the doctor checked Sybil. He sighed. When he finished, he looked at Charlotte.

"It is not good, I am afraid. Lady Fallow's fever must break by early morning. If it does not, well, I fear for her. I suggest keeping her cool. If she comes around, she must drink tepid tea or have some port."

He walked away out of the room, with Dollie and Mrs. Wilks following. Curious, Charlotte tried to hear what they were saying, and frustratingly could only make out some words; loss, children, guilt, burden...

What were they discussing? Why were they whispering? Charlotte had a mind to question them, but Sybil stirred, saying something. The doctor then came back in.

"Lay cold compressed towels on her forehead. It will bring out the heat. I will take leave now and come back in the morning to check on her."

"I suggest you stay until the storm is over," Mrs. Wilks said looking outside. "It seems to be worse."

"Perhaps you are right," said the doctor. "It may be a better idea for me to stay the night, then I can keep an eye on her ladyship."

"I'll have the guest room made up for you."

That night, Charlotte stayed awake, keeping her mother cool as advised. She told the doctor she would call for him if her mother's condition worsened. The fire was put out and the room cooled down. But still Sybil's body shook with the fever. Charlotte tried to fight the sleep from her eyes as she kept changing the flannel on Sybil's forehead. She didn't know when she fell asleep or when Dollie and Mrs. Wilks took over caring for Sybil.

Charlotte woke up to a new morning. Bright sunlight streamed in. She found herself sleeping in Sybil's bed, who was sitting up next to her, sipping something from a cup.

"Mama!" she exclaimed, hugging her. "You are awake!" She felt Sybil's forehead. "Your fever has broken. Oh, Mama."

"Yes, darling. My fever has broken, and I must be grateful to you, and everybody else. I am grateful to God to let me see you again. I am truly blessed." Sybil's voice was exhausted.

"Indeed, you are, Mama. But you will only rest now and do nothing else. You are still weak," Charlotte said.

Sybil laughed softly. "As you wish, my love."

OVER THE NEXT FEW DAYS, Charlotte kept a watchful eye on her mother who seemed to be a little brighter. But then, a shadow would cross her face. Sybil still felt chilled most days and slept a lot, which worried Charlotte.

"Mama, if something is worrying you, you would tell me?" she asked, as she combed Sybil's hair. Charlotte wanted to look after her mother herself. She didn't want to leave Sybil for one minute.

"Of course, I would, my dear child. But I do not want you to fret about me. And I fear you are missing out on seeing your friends. It is not good for you to spend all the time with me."

"After that awful night, I thought I had lost you. And I cannot bear it. The doctor said there is nothing more he can do for you, and the only way forward is to rest."

"I will rest and get better. Now, my dear, help me lie down in my bed."

As Sybil went to stand from the side of the bed, she suddenly slumped forward and fell. Charlotte's heart stopped when Sybil didn't open her eyes. She shouted for help, and immediately a footman entered with Dollie. They helped Sybil onto the bed. When Charlotte splashed water on Sybil's face, she stirred.

"Let her sleep," whispered Dollie. "She is exhausted."

The look of disturb on Dollie's face made Charlotte worry further.

"Dollie, please tell me the truth. What is worrying my mother that is making her so ill?"

"As I believe it, I am certain she is not worrying about anything," said Dollie, avoiding Charlotte's eyes. "Why do you believe so?"

"Why do you not look at me? What is this secret? What is my

mother hiding from me? I am certain you know of it. I can only ask you, Dollie. Will you not lighten my heart?"

"My dear Lady Charlotte, I assure you there is no mystery," Dollie said in soothing voice. "Now, I will look after your mother while she sleeps. Go and do something which will amuse you. I am certain your mother would wish it."

"No, I want to stay," said Charlotte.

"If her ladyship becomes ill further, I will come and fetch you. Now, go."

Charlotte reluctantly left Dollie, disappointed that she received no answer to her questions. As she walked to the library, a memory was triggered where she saw the groomsman talking to her mother one evening. She was watching from her window and could only see a little. But she saw her mother's frightened face. Was he the reason why she had withered away, almost losing her life?

"A LETTER FOR LADY FALLOW."

"Thank you, Mr. Donaldson. I will see that Mama receives it," said Charlotte. The butler stayed where he was. "Is there anything else?"

"Yes, Lady Charlotte, there is. I wanted to say since the day you arrived, you have brought much joy to your mother and to everyone in the household. If you ever need anything from me, or Mrs. Wilks, you only need to ask."

"That is rather kind of you." Charlotte was surprised. "I am very grateful. However, there is one thing. What were you talking about with Dollie and Mrs. Wilks on the night the doctor visited? I feel like everyone is hiding some rather important information from me."

Just like Dollie, the butler seemed uncomfortable and fidgeted.

"Mr. Donaldson?"

"Lady Charlotte, there is no secret or important information that we are keeping from you."

"But –" began Charlotte.

"I must leave. Duty calls."

With a sigh, Charlotte picked up the envelope and turned it in her hand. She looked at the address, it was her papa's country estate where he was now spending most of his time.

This is a letter for Mama. However, she is in no fit state to read it. Charlotte was afraid the letter would further upset her if her father had written something damning. Without another second's thought, Charlotte tore the envelope open and took out the parchment.

Sybil,

I am writing to inform you I will no longer be residing at the London house. We both know we are not compatible with one another, and we do not require to see each other on a regular basis. You will still receive money every month, and the household expenditure will be continuously paid as well. However, I do not want to see you or Charlotte again. When I come to visit the house, I wish you and Charlotte to be elsewhere. I will inform you via letter before I arrive.

Irvin

Charlotte scrunched the letter up in a ball and threw it into the fireplace. She watched the flames lick the letter, burning it greedily. She could not let her mother read it. No, she must spare her.

She wished her father was not so unfair and uncaring toward her mother, his wife. What had she done that was so awful to make him dislike her? It was true her own relationship with him had suffered as she grew up, and now it would never become better for her father refused to see them again. Oh, how cruel he was. If only Dwight were here; she wanted to talk to him, to lay out her woes. She wished fervently for him.

CHAPTER 17

Dwight entered the drawing room where Charlotte was playing a melancholy tune on the pianoforte, making her stop abruptly.

"My dear Charlotte! Everyone is talking about your father. I'm so very sorry. Such a scandal. I could not let you to bear it alone."

He took her in his arms and held her tightly. Then realising his actions, he let her go. "I do apologise. I do not know what came over me."

Charlotte, feeling warm under his gaze, allowed herself to lift her eyes to his. They were full of concern. He was obviously talking about her father's affairs and his refusal to live with his legal family. Of course, the gossipers had prevailed. It was no secret.

"Dwight, I am so glad you are here. I have felt very alone, and that is the truth. Mama is unwell, and sometimes I fear she may die. There is too much sadness in this household."

"Let us go for a promenade in the garden, dearest. It is a beautiful day of sunshine—why stay inside?"

"We will need a chaperone," Charlotte said, remembering the last time they were together.

"Very well," said Dwight. "I shall wait in the hall."

The maid walked behind Charlotte and Dwight in the estate garden. The flowers were in full bloom, but Charlotte had no care for their vibrancy and brilliant fragrance. Her heart ached for her mother.

"What is it you are fretting about?" Dwight asked.

"I am just fretting. It is nothing serious," she said, trying to alleviate his concern. "But thank you, Mr. Calverton, for asking. I fear my countenance is too telling."

"I would be glad if you call me Dwight as you did when we were children. It is all right, is it not that I call you Charlotte?"

Charlotte smiled. "I love it so."

"Charlotte, you are very dear to me." He paused and for a moment, she thought he looked nervous. But what possible reason could there be for nervousness? They had been dear friends for as long as she could remember.

He cleared his throat and continued, "Dearest Charlotte, I am in love with you. I cannot be with anyone else. I wonder if you would you do me the honour of having me as your husband?"

Charlotte's heart lurched. She had not expected this. It was, of course, delightful and joyful. But she had to think of her mother.

She smiled at him with tears in her eyes. "Dwight, how wonderful it is to hear those words. And I also have a confession." She felt her cheeks grow warm. "I have loved you since we were children. It was different then, of course. But I cannot tell you enough how joyful you have made me feel. But shouldn't our parents agree or arrange this?"

"In time. We can certainly wait until all is in order. I hope you do not meet anyone else. I could not bear it."

Charlotte laughed with delight. She wished she could place her hand on his, but it would not be appropriate. And dearest Lord, she did not want another scandal attached to her family.

"I could never be with anyone else, Dwight, apart from you. Do not worry, for my heart will always be yours."

They continued to walk. Charlotte's joy waned some as she thought of her mother.

"What is it, my love?" Dwight asked. "You have said it's nothing, but something is causing you to worry."

"I know this will sound ... wrong. Please, do not laugh at me. But I believe the reason my mother's health has deteriorated is because of our new groomsman." And then she told Dwight what she saw that day.

Dwight did not laugh at her; instead, his face clouded, and she saw the seriousness with which he took her thoughts. "I shall visit him at once. I shall not let him upset you or Lady Fallow anymore."

"No, Dwight, please do not go," she said, suddenly panicked. "I may be mistaken. if I am, then we will both look foolish. I will investigate him first. I must know what he said to Mama."

"No, Charlotte. I want to help. Let me handle this."

But Charlotte was determined. If the groomsman was the reason her mother was sick, she would tell Dwight and perhaps together, they could make certain he would go away for a very long time.

THE WIND WHISTLED that night and sheets of rain came and went. Why had Mr. Harrison been called away? What was so urgent? Duncan wondered. Later, he found out that Lady Fallow had a fever and needed a doctor. If she made it to the next morning, she would live.

This was not good. He needed her to live, because she was the only one who would pay him his monthly 'wages' as he liked to call them. The cottage his mother had rented all these years was behind; he couldn't keep up with the rent payments. His siblings all had different lives, now, and he rarely saw any of them.

He would soon be poorer than ever before. He may not even have a house any longer. His dire future soured his stomach. So, that night, he waited for news of Lady Fallow's health. He didn't sleep well, tossing and turning all night, dreaming that she would be dead before long.

Eventually he gave up trying to sleep and paced the floor of the cottage, fearing the worst. He drank ale, but that didn't calm his heart. He didn't care if she died really, it was the money he was after. In the turmoil of his mind, he thought of his last conversation with Michael.

"What do ye want?"

"Can't I talk to me brother?" Michael looked around the house. "Wha' 'appened to tha furniture here?"

"Sold it."

"To pay for ya gamblin?" Michael sat on a wooden box.

"What's it ta ya?" said Duncan.

"Look, we're all tryin' here. I wanna 'elp. You're me big brother, ain't ya? The others are worried too. We 'eard you're deep in trouble."

"That's my problem, Mike. Anyway, I thought ya said ya all didn't want me when Mum died? No one's ever around anymore."

"Well, that was because we all was upset. We miss ya, Dunc. 'specially Katie. Ya know, Mum wouldn't want this, to see you in such a state."

"So, where is Katie? Why ain't she come and seen me, then? Where is she? She ain't never here." Duncan avoided the subject of his mother. He still loved her, and the thought of her gone caused him to feel sick and alone.

"Katie got a job as a scullery maid, ain't that grand? She'll come when she's got time off. The others are doing good, too. I got Albert a job with me at the shipyard. It's good work. But I 'eard you work at the stables now as a groomsman, at the big estate."

"Aye," said Duncan.

"Does it pay well?"

Duncan shrugged. "It's all right. Keeps me goin'," he lied. He would never tell his brother he was struggling.

"Come an' see us, Dunc. This visitin' goes both ways. We see each other ever' month on our days off. At a pub. I'll leave the 'ddress with ya, all right?"

Again, Duncan shrugged. "If ya want."

"See ya, Dunc."

Duncan wasn't stupid, he knew the real reason of his brother's visit. They all wanted to know who this Sally was; it was the one thing that was haunting them. He would tell them one day when the time was right. But not anytime soon. He might go and see them anyway; he missed them too. When dawn came, he learned Lady Fallow had come out of her fever. It was good news to him.

DUNCAN STRUCK A MATCH. He watched the splint burn, casting a little illumination in the dark alley. It burnt his finger. Cursing, he let the match fall into the small puddle where it sizzled. He lit another one, and this time he used it to light his cigarette. It had been a long day at the stables. Mr. Harrison didn't give him a break. One of the horses was pregnant, ready to give birth to a new foal soon. He was told to keep a close eye on her, but to not go to her.

He did keep an eye on her, and at the same time, he had kept an eye on the house and the activity. Duncan saw a carriage approach the house and decided to see who it was. He turned his attention from the horse; she would be all right for a bit. He sprinted across to the grounds and waited in the shadows. To his disappointment, he didn't see who went inside the house, but then a little later, someone came out with Charlotte. Duncan recognised him at once; he was the one with her when she collided with him that day. He was sure of it. He wondered if they were courting. He saw them go to the gardens, but he couldn't follow them. He had to get back to the stables before Mr. Harrison found him missing from his duties. He couldn't afford to lose this job.

But now, the day was over, and another night of gambling awaited him. He sat on a tin drum waiting to be let into the place where they all gathered. At last, the door opened, and he was told to get in, quickly.

He followed the man into a dimly lit room. Cigar smoke swirled around two lit candles that were almost at their ends. Duncan took a chair with four others. They were an odd bunch, and much older than he was. His old friend from the shipyard had introduced him to them; he was here, too.

"Well, well. Where 'ave ya been all this time, Duncan?" asked the ringleader, Stuart. "Did ya bring the money ya owe?"

Stuart was a thin, short man. Everyone was terrified of him. He would not be crossed by anyone. If they tried, well, that would be the last time. Duncan didn't want to be on the wrong side of him.

"I 'ave the money," Duncan said. He put his hand in his pocket and took out a wad of notes, placing it before Stuart. His mouth was dry, and he wished he had an ale in his hand. But he daren't ask. Stuart took the money and counted it greedily.

"All right, it's all there. Now, you can play some more. I 'ope you have more."

The other men sniggered, including his old friend.

"Yeah, I 'ave it," said Duncan, irritated. He took out the last of it and laid it out on the table. He was planning to win that night.

Stuart grinned and gave Duncan a tankard of ale. Gratefully, Duncan took a big gulp. The game began. It wasn't long before any money Duncan had, was gone. And now, he was in debt all over again.

"Oh, bad luck, Dunc," said Stuart. "An' now, you owe more to us."

"I'll get it, I promise," said Duncan.

"Yeah, 'ow?"

"You... You can 'ave Lady Fallow's carriage. I'll take it from her, I will."

Stuart began to laugh, slowly at first, and then very loudly. The others joined in. Duncan laughed nervously.

"I like tha'! An' I like ya," Stuart said to Duncan. He slapped him on the back. "I'll wait for the carriage, then."

Duncan left the house, his heart beating fast. What had he done? Why did he promise something impossible? And how was he going to get the carriage? He needed a plan, and very quickly.

He would have to demand it from Lady Fallow.

CHAPTER 18

DUNCAN FOUND Sybil sitting quietly on a bench in the garden. It was a good time to approach her as she was alone. He crept behind her, and unintentionally stepped on a twig. The sound of the crack alerted Sybil.

"What do you want?" she stood up, placing her hand on her heart.

"Dun't worry, M' Lady," Duncan smiled. "I just come to sor' ou' some business." Duncan took the empty space on the bench and leaned back. He lit a cigarette.

"I wish you to put that out," Sybil said in a shaky voice. "I do not allow it in my garden."

"All right," said Duncan, and put it out immediately. He had to get on her good side. "So, I 'ave come for more money."

"Did I not tell you last time there is no more? I have sold everything I could. I have nothing left."

"I dunt believe ya. Ya live in a big 'ouse, and you dunt have enough to sell?"

"I have informed you already. What I could sell is all gone."

"There is one thing you have tha' I want." Duncan grinned.

"What is that?"

"One of yer carriages. They'll fetch a fine penny, won't they? Yer dunt 'ave to sell them, I 'ave someone who will do it. All yer 'ave ta do is give one to me."

Sybil took in a long and hard breath. "I will never give one to you. No, it is not possible."

"You're forgetting what I can do, M' Lady. I'll tell everyone about yer dear daughter, my sista. And ye know what'll 'appen then. Do yer want to take tha' risk?"

"Please just leave us alone. Charlotte is everything to me. I cannot bear it if she found out and left me."

"I dunt care. I only wan' da carriage. 'Ave it ready, I'll come and take it at night."

"What is going on here?" a voice boomed somewhere among the shrubs.

Dwight, along with Charlotte, appeared from behind it. Dwight narrowed his eyes at Duncan.

"*You*. The groomsman, is it not? Why are you here? Are you harassing Lady Fallow?"

"I 'ave said what I wanted ta. I'll let La'y Fallow tell yer all abou' it." Duncan glanced at Charlotte, and his grin vanished. It was as if his mother was standing right before him; her presence hit him hard. "I 'ave ta go!"

***

"Mama, what was the groomsman doing here?" asked Charlotte when they all were back in the house.

Dwight had politely excused himself, for which she was grateful. Sybil was once more feeling unwell and was shaking. Charlotte sat her down on the bed, allowing her to rest her head on her shoulder. She didn't notice the door was slightly ajar or that there was a footman standing outside, listening.

"Mama, will you tell me what the groomsman was doing in the garden? What did he say to you to make you so ill?"

"I cannot tell you, my dear. It will only hurt you," sighed Sybil.

"But you must. I believe he is the reason for your ill health. Am I correct or am I wrong?"

Sybil lifted her head. "I cannot bear this burden any longer. I believe I must tell you, my dear."

To Charlotte's astonishment, there were tears in her mother's eyes. "Please, tell me."

"What I have to tell you will be quite shocking, so I want you to be alert. Do not judge me for I was desperate, and I wanted a child."

Charlotte didn't understand—what had her dear mother done? But she didn't ask and instead waited for her to tell her story.

"Before you arrived, my love, I had four stillborn children. They were all girls. With every stillborn, your father was more disappointed with me. But he did not know about the last stillbirth. When he was away, I had Dollie search for a newborn child for me immediately."

With her heart beating rapidly, Charlotte heard her mother tell her the tale of her grief as if she were in a faraway place. Charlotte didn't feel this was real. She was taken from a woman who just had given birth to her? She wasn't a real Fallow; she wasn't a real lady at all?

Was this why she had always felt so different to all the other women of society? She gulped and her mind spun. Her life was beginning to make sense to her now. She felt so much empathy for the common people because she *was one*. It was why she liked to spend time with the household staff as a child.

Her pulse quickened as the truth of it washed over her.

"But if Papa does not know the truth about me, why will he not love me?" Her voice was unsteady as she tried not to let her emotions take over. She had to be strong and think clearly. She wanted to know everything.

"Your papa never wanted a girl. If you had been a boy, he would have been delighted. However, I have loved you since the day you came to me. I shall never forget when Dollie placed you in my arms." When Sybil tried to put a hand to Charlotte's face, Charlotte stood up and backed away.

"I cannot believe you took me away from my mother. How she must have felt..."

"Oh, darling, it is true I did something very wrong, and I believe I will repent for it one day. But we paid her handsomely. She had her reasons to give you away—we did not make her do it. Charlotte, she was struggling to feed another child."

Charlotte's lips parted as she tried to imagine the scene. Her shock gave way to sudden anger.

"That is no excuse, Mama. You took away her child to make it your own. Do you know where she is now? Where this mama is?" Charlotte's eyes were dark with pain. She wrung her hands in frustration and disbelief.

"I do not know where she is, Charlotte. But there is one man who will know. The groomsman, Duncan. He... He is your brother. Please forgive me for not telling you sooner. He has been blackmailing me for money. He said he would tell everyone about your real birth if I failed to do what he wanted—"

Charlotte went stiff. "Are there any other secrets you have kept from me?" Her tone was harsh, but right then, she could not feel anything but shock and anger.

"I have told you everything," said Sybil. "Will you leave me now you know the truth? That is what I have feared for months and months."

"I-I do not know what to think. I n-need to be alone." Charlotte ran out of the room, tears coming rapidly.

"Lady Charlotte, what is the matter?" asked Dollie who was walking her way.

Charlotte stopped and stared at her mother's lady's maid. "You were part of all this, were you not? You knew about me from the beginning. Who else knew? I feel I do not know you anymore. I do not know anyone."

"Wh-What is it?" Dollie asked. But Charlotte could tell from her expression that she knew full well what was going on.

"You already know!" Charlotte jolted away to go to her bedchambers.

She lay on her bed, her stomach churning. How could they do this to her? What a cruel thing to be taken away from her own mother whom she may not ever meet or know. She had a brother... Duncan – the groomsman – he had been kind to her. She understood why now, but was her mother telling her the truth? Had he blackmailed her mother for money? If so, it proved he was not a nice man at all.

Did she want a brother like him? Dear Lord. What kind of person was he? And what kind of person was she? She had no idea anymore. Charlotte knew she must have a conversation with him, and that it would indeed be painful. But she had to know who her real family was, who her mother and father were, and did she have other siblings?

She had to go and see Duncan.

NATURALLY, the footman had heard it all. Lady Charlotte was not Lady Fallow's child; she was a commoner. Oh, what a scandal this was to be. Immediately, he went downstairs and revealed his discovery to everyone. There was a stunned response, but then there was the excitement of true gossip.

From some there were exclamations and words said that made Lady Fallow unworthy of their respect. For others, there was sympathy. They understood their employer's desperation, for they had witnessed three stillbirths. They had seen how withdrawn Lord Fallow had become from his duty as a husband, and how he had become cruel and distant.

"What is going on here?" The butler came into the servant's hall, followed by Mrs. Wilks.

"Tom told us about Lady Fallow's scandal," a young maid who had just joined told the butler, unaware of her foolishness.

The butler lifted an eyebrow. "And what scandal would that be?"

"That Lady Charlotte ain't her real daughter," the maid replied.

There was a gasp from Mrs. Wilks, and the butler's face went pale, but to his credit, he recovered immediately.

"This gossip is to not leave this house, and no one must repeat it. I hope this is clear."

"Is it true, then?" asked another footman.

"True or not, I want to hear no more of this. Lady Charlotte is Lady Fallow's daughter, as far as I am concerned. and as far as you all are concerned. Lady Charlotte is a Fallow. Now, get back to work, all of you. And remember, I want not one word said if you want to keep your positions."

The butler and the housekeeper went to their office.

"Dear Lord in heaven," Mr. Donaldson said.

"I know," said Mrs. Wilks. They both sank into chairs. Then she rang the bell, and a maid came in.

"Will you bring tea please, Abby."

When the tea arrived shortly, Mrs. Wilks poured a cup for her and the butler.

"What do you think will happen now?" she asked.

"I do not know. I feel sorry for Lady Fallow and Lady Charlotte. You are aware this story will not stay here. It will spread like wildfire."

"Indeed," said Mrs. Wilks. She took a long sip of her hot tea. "Let us pray things will not be as bad as they seem now. And that Lord Fallow does not find out."

"Amen to that," said the butler.

CHAPTER 19

"I DO NOT WANT you to see Lady Charlotte anymore, Dwight." Lady Calverton stood in the drawing room, looking out the window. They were at their townhouse, which was opposite Hyde Park. Carriages went in and out of the entrance on this fine day.

"Why not?" Dwight asked, alarmed that his mother already knew what he was planning. He was sitting on the sofa, knowing what his mother was going to say. But he would play along.

"You know very well why I ask you to listen to me." Lady Calverton turned to face him, her lips thin and her nose pointed in its normal haughty way. "The scandal of that house is all over the *ton*. We cannot and must not associate ourselves with them."

"What scandal do you speak of?" asked Dwight, dreading what was to come. He had only found out the news recently himself, but he continued on. "I have heard of none."

"Of course, you have, and you are very aware that Charlotte is not a Fallow. She is not Lady Charlotte, but a mere commoner." His mother's tone was like a startled crow.

"Mama, it is hardly her fault she was taken when she was a child. She is very much a lady to me, and hardly a commoner. She is well spoken, has beautiful music skills, sings excellently, has poise, and shows etiquette like a woman of society. If you ask me, she is flawless. If you want to compare her to some of the other ladies of the *ton*, then I am quite happy to speak of the flaws of these other women you wish me to marry. And I shall not marry them. When the time comes, I shall only marry Lady Charlotte."

"The one you want to marry is no better than a mere beggar on the street. She will have no dowry. It has come to my knowledge that Lord Fallow has moved out of his London home and now resides at his country estate. I am certain he will have disowned his wife and Lady Charlotte now the scandal is out. They will have nowhere to go."

Dwight heard the subdued delight in his mother's voice; it irked him that he had a mother like her. But he kept his head clear. He didn't want to have a quarrel with her.

"I believe if it comes to that, I will ask them to stay in my cottage by the sea," he told her calmly.

"You will do no such thing. That cottage was given to you by your grandfather."

"Mama, Grandfather was a kind and generous man. If you remember, he once worked as a clerk in his earlier life being the third son of an earl. He understands what work is. So, he would not mind whom I let into my own cottage. Now, I do not wish to carry on with this conversation. I have spoken with Papa about Lady Charlotte, and he has no qualms about me wanting to marry her."

"Your father has always had a generous amount of pity for that girl," Lady Calverton said dismissively.

"It is not pity, but love and adoration. He was most delighted when I spoke of my decision. Now, Mama, I will leave. It has been interesting conversing with you as always. I shall see myself out."

Dwight climbed into his carriage and told the driver to take him to the Fallow estate. He had heard the gossip and was rather sad at first that Charlotte hadn't told him herself. But after some thinking, he realised she may have only just found out herself. How shocking it surely was for her to know she was not Lady Fallow's real daughter. But he did not feel differently about her. He loved her still.

He wanted to tell her she would always have a place in his heart and in his home. Charlotte needed someone to be by her side, to be her support, and he would be that for her. His mother could not stop him from seeing her.

CHARLOTTE DIDN'T KNOW what to do. Should she go and see the groomsman, her brother? It did seem odd to think of him as that for she had no brother growing up. She certainly liked the idea of having one, but she had to remind herself what Duncan was like—that he blackmailed her mother—her *adoptive* mother. She sighed deeply and drew in a long breath. However she thought about it, Sybil would always be her mother because she loved her. Charlotte understood why she did what she did and now felt empathy for her.

Charlotte realised Sybil only had her and no one else. Charlotte could never abandon her. But first she had to know of her original family, and if she had to face her brother to know the truth, she would do it.

She marched up to the stables and straight up to him.

"Lady Charlotte, do you want me take your horse out for you?" Duncan asked.

"No. I want to speak to you of what is bothering me. You know I am not Lady Fallow's daughter. I would like it if you would drop the pretence."

His face turned dark, and Charlotte flinched.

"So, the lady told you the truth then?" He laughed, a mean tone in his voice. "I didn't think she 'ad it in 'er."

"So, it is true you are my brother?"

Duncan stroked the mane of the horse he was attending. "It is true. You are my youngest sister. Mum named ya Sally."

"Did you know I was given away for money?"

"Not at first, but you looked so much like Mum, I 'ad suspicions. I asked her, and she told me about yer."

"How did you feel about it, after learning the truth?" Charlotte wanted to know everything.

"What do yer think? I was angry, I was. I couldn't believe Mum would do it, send her child away because she couldn't feed one more."

"How do you mean? What about your father, did he not help?"

"Our father?" Duncan laughed again. "He upped and left when you were just born. Not seen 'im since. I think he came back once, but Mum sent 'im packing. She wanted none of him."

"Where is she? Where is the woman to whom I was born?" asked Charlotte. "I want to see her."

"You can't. She's dead."

That was a shock to Charlotte, she hadn't thought of her birth mother as gone.

She drew in a sharp breath and stood a moment, taking it in. Then she asked, "Do I have other brothers and sisters?"

"Aye, there are a few of us, but they are somewhere in London working or somethin'. I 'aven't seem them for a while." Then Duncan's eyes softened. "I woulda liked ya as a sista, you know. When Mum told me you were sent 'ere, I was angry, I was. I thought it unfair you got the luxury, the good life when we all 'ad to work 'ard."

"That was why you took money from Lady Fallow?" said Charlotte.

"And now, thanks to her, I won't get anymore. I'll be dead by next week, I will, if I don't give 'em the carriage I promised."

"Why would you be dead?"

"It's nothin'. You'd better go," Duncan mumbled.

"If I let you have the carriage, will you leave us alone? I do not want you to ask for any more money again. And if you do, I will send you to prison. I love my mother very much, and I want her to be well again. Do I have your promise? And know, Duncan, that I mean it. Every word."

He gazed at her, and his eyes narrowed. Finally, he took a long breath. "Yes, all right."

"And you shall leave employment and find another position elsewhere. I will ask Mr. Harrison to write you a good reference. And do not fret, I will not disclose your actions to anyone."

Charlotte hoped this closed the business with Duncan, and now her mother could become well again.

DUNCAN DRANK MANY tankards of ale that evening. He thought about Charlotte. How could he feel so small in front of his little sister? Over the months since he knew who she was, he had begun to feel like he really knew her and had become fond of her in a way, despite his hard heart. But she was still a Fallow even though she was born in a poor house. She had her life, and he had his, though Duncan didn't care for his. Yet he was relieved his sister had given him the carriage. He was disappointed he wouldn't get any more money from Lady Fallow.

"Mum, you would be proud of your youngest daughter," he spoke to the ceiling. "That Sally ... no, that Charlotte Fallow is a kind-hearted girl. But if you knew what I've done, you'd hate me, just like everyone else. But it ain't my fault. I needed the money. I wish you was alive. I-I miss you." He was feeling sorry for himself. He had done a horrible thing to Lady Fallow. Still, he was not to blame for everything.

He hiccupped and drank more ale, passing out eventually. Unbeknownst to him, Michael had heard every word he'd uttered to their dead mother, and he now knew Charlotte Fallow was their sister.

Duncan also didn't know Michael put him into his bed and stayed with him all night.

CHAPTER 20

"Is this who you choose, Dwight? You choose that girl over me?" Lady Calverton's words sliced through the fraught air.

"Now dearest, do not deny your son the one he loves. Lady Charlotte is a lovely soul, and I am quite fond of her, too. If Dwight is inclined to marry her when she is of age, I see no objection." Lord Calverton tried to pacify his wife, who pretended to wipe away a tear.

"That girl is no lady. She is a commoner, as you are aware. Everyone in the *ton* is talking about the scandal of what her mother has done. To swap a dead child for one from a family of commoners. How horrendous!"

"Mama, do not speak of it in such a manner." Dwight stood up from his chair. He detested this kind of conversation and wished it would stop being repeated. "It was no fault of Lady Charlotte that she was dealt such a hand, and we must have kindness toward Lady Fallow for initiating such an action. The poor woman was helpless, and after four stillbirths, she perhaps thought she had no choice."

"Is that what that *girl* told you?" his mother asked scornfully. "Of course, it must be so. She is no better than her mother."

"Lady Charlotte is a kind soul, as Papa has said. She did not inform me of the news, and never you mind who told me." Dwight turned to Lord Calverton. "Papa, do I have your blessing in pursuing Lady Charlotte?"

"Yes, my dearest son. You have my blessing."

"Why do you choose to disrespect me so?" Lady Calverton wouldn't give up. "I do feel faint. All this drama is not good for my health." She put the back of her hand on her forehead and leaned against a chair.

"I wish you wouldn't be so dramatic, dear," Lord Calverton said mildly. "If you wish, you are free to go to your chambers and lie down. I will go with our son to the Fallow estate for I wish to see the child myself. I daresay Lord Fallow will still be vacant. I pity the man."

"I believe enough has been said now, Papa. Let us leave."

So, father and son left a rather disgusted mother and wife as they left the house to get into their carriage.

"I SHALL COME FOR A SHORT WHILE," said Lord Calverton. "But then I must leave for Hampshire, for I have a meeting. And I urge you to be gentle with Lady Charlotte when you converse with her."

Lady Fallow seemed to be frailer since the last time they had visited, and it was obvious it was the scandal that had taken a toll on her health. The poor woman was paler and seemed completely melancholy.

"It is very kind of you to come and visit," Sybil smiled wanly. "We do not have many visitors now."

There was an understandable silence, and then Lord Calverton spoke.

"I will not hide why we are here, Lady Fallow. And I'm afraid all I can do is extend my respect to you. What you have gone through is most unfortunate, and I cannot imagine how you are feeling. I wanted to come and say we are still your friends, and should you need any help, we will do our utter best to accommodate your needs."

"You are very kind, and I may take you up on your word if such an event occurs," Sybil said.

"Now, my young lady, let me see you," Lord Calverton smiled turning to Charlotte. "What a pleasure it is to be in your company once again. I do wish I had a daughter like you."

"You are very kind," Charlotte blushed. Dwight caught her eye and smiled.

"Charlotte has come a long way since your last visit." Sybil's tone echoed how proud she was. She seemed delighted with the turn of subject. "Her skills in playing the pianoforte are rather splendid. And she is becoming rather learned in the arts and geography."

"Oh, Mama." Charlotte blushed a deeper red. "You do exaggerate. Lord Calverton, I do not believe I play as well as Mama claims. In fact, I am perhaps mediocre."

"Do not believe her, Papa. I have had the privilege of hearing her music, and it is more than good. I say it is rather excellent," said Dwight.

"Then I would like to listen to this wonderful skill you have, Lady Charlotte."

"What a jolly idea that is," exclaimed Dwight, who also seemed delighted with the change of focus.

"Do go on," Sybil coaxed her. "You play so well."

"All right." Charlotte sat on the stool and placed her nimble fingers on the keys. She closed her eyes.

She pressed the keys, and the music came with ease. Dwight sensed her every breath and heartbeat, which seemed to echo the rhythm. He closed his eyes and became lost in the melody. He wished he was sitting next to her, enjoying the piece of music beside her. When she stopped, he opened his eyes, feeling much disappointed. But he would have other chances to hear her play he was certain.

After much applause, Lord Calverton declared he must leave and thanked his hosts for a wonderful afternoon.

"Will you not stay for tea?" asked Sybil.

"When the time is right, I shall with pleasure. But I have a meeting to attend to in Hertfordshire. Dwight will stay for a while if you allow. I will be back tomorrow morning."

"It would be delightful to have his company," said Sybil.

Dwight and Charlotte shared a private look of love and friendship.

THEY SAT TOGETHER in the veranda overlooking the setting sun. Sybil left them to be together with a drowsy chaperone sitting on the other side of the veranda.

"I cannot tell you how concerned I am about the news," Dwight said.

"I was ... taken aback to learn of it," Charlotte admitted. "Upset and even angry at first. However, I cannot change what has taken place already and neither can Mama. I was quite irate with her when she confessed, but I now think I understand why she did it."

Dwight grabbed her hand and squeezed it.

"I have met my brother," continued Charlotte. "He is the groomsman."

"That explains many things," said Dwight. "I can hardly believe it."

Charlotte nodded. "It was a shock to me as well to learn of it. He blackmailed Mama for money, threatening to tell everyone about me. It was what made Mama so ill. But he has left employment now as I requested. With him gone, I hope Mama will recover soon. Dwight, I feel there is more to her ill health, and I do wonder what else it could be."

"Have you spoken to her about it?"

Charlotte shook her head. "I do not want her to fret anymore—it could be the undoing of her. I only want her to become better, and nothing else matters."

Dwight took Charlotte's other hand in his, and she let him. She marvelled at how his touch could still her aching heart.

"I want to marry you when you become of age, Charlotte. I love you, and no one else will do. That has not changed."

"Oh, Dwight..." Charlotte murmured. She felt his hands warm hers, and she began to weep. "I love you, but I cannot marry you."

"Why ever not?" Dwight released her. "We are meant to be together."

"I cannot let the scandal of my family, or my true heritage taint your lineage. I am not a real lady, but a commoner, you know that." Her eyes brimmed with tears.

"All that matters not to me, my dearest love." He touched the back of his hand over her cheeks, wiping away the tears. "I take you for who you are, not for your status. Father agrees with me."

"And your mother? I do not want to break up your family."

Dwight sighed. "Mother is against our alliance, but I do not care. I have chosen you, and she can like it or not. Do not push me away, my dear, for it is only you I ever loved."

"And I have always loved you, too," Charlotte whispered.

"Do you know how you two have ruined me?" Irvin roared. "I am the joke of all London."

He paced up and down the drawing room. Sybil was glad Charlotte wasn't in the room with them. She was not at all surprised to see him; in truth, she had been waiting for him. She was too weak to argue, and so she stayed silent.

"I am being made a mockery. To believe Charlotte was my own!" Irvin continued roaring. "I always knew she was different, and not one of us. It is her face. She looks nothing like me or you. And you, Sybil, how could you even think of acting on such a thing as... I cannot even speak of it! What did you do with the fourth dead child? Bury it with the others?"

"Irvin, I had no choice. I wanted to make you happy..."

"Then why did you not find a boy? You knew I wanted a boy, and perhaps then we could have been a family. I could have begun to love you again."

He sat down, pushing his hands through his hair. He stared at Sybil.

"I want you and that girl gone from his house. You can take Dollie, too, for I understand she was part of your plan, was she not?"

"But where would we go? You cannot do this, Irvin. Please, have some sympathy for Charlotte. She is innocent of this. It was not her fault," Sybil cried.

"I do not care for that girl, and I never have. You and she will leave the estate. I will arrange a small cottage, which I believe is quite generous of me given what you have done to me and my reputation. You will have a small allowance a year. I shall not divorce you for how much of a scandal can the Fallow estate take?" Irvin laughed as a mad person. "Have your things packed by tomorrow morn."

"What will we do?" Charlotte rushed in as soon as Irvin had left. "I heard it all in the hall."

"I do not know, my dearest. Perhaps it is best we do leave the estate. Lord Fallow has been kind enough to let us have a cottage and some money. I cannot ask for more."

Sybil hugged her daughter as they both cried in each other's arms.

CHAPTER 21

Charlotte rode through the estate, going faster and faster. She had to get out of the house where there was nothing but sadness. It was her fault that the man she thought was her father, Lord Fallow, had disowned her and the one person she had loved since she could remember, her mother. Of course, Lady Fallow would always be her mother, even though Charlotte had been taken from another woman. She would never know her birth mother, and that was sad, too. But she wouldn't think of that, for it did not change anything.

She was sorry that it had come to this, that she and her mother would have to leave the estate, for the Fallow estate had been her home her entire life. Sybil was also melancholy to leave. But there was nothing she could say that would change his mind. So, they would move and live a life away, as modestly as possible.

Charlotte galloped under overhanging trees and crossed a bridge over a stream where she finally stopped. The morning sun disappeared behind dark clouds, threatening rain. But Charlotte didn't care so much about that. She dismounted and sat against a tree, feeling helpless and wondering what their future would be like. Would their friends, Anne and her mother, still be their allies or would they rebuff them, too, as most of society certainly had already done. And poor Dollie, it was not her fault she followed orders from her mother, why was she being punished? It was so unfair.

A cooler wind blew around her, and Charlotte placed her arms around her knees. She was unaware a carriage had stopped on the path behind her and who came to stand by her before she looked up.

"Anne!" she gasped.

"I thought it was you," Anne said. She sat beside Charlotte on the blanket Charlotte had spread. "I went to your house, and the butler informed me you went for a ride. I have heard the dreadful news, my dear."

Anne took Charlotte's hand and kissed her cheek.

"Is this all true then? You are not Lady Fallow's daughter?"

"It is true—I cannot lie," said Charlotte, feeling tears fill her eyes. She blinked them away. "She may not be my birth mother, but she will always be my mama. I suppose you will not want to be friends with me now."

"I do not care for that, dearest. You and I will always be friends, and I will defy anyone who tries to stop me. Even if it is my own mama."

"Oh, you must not do that, Anne. Not for me."

"What will become of you? Will Lord Fallow accept you?"

"I am afraid not. He has disowned me and Mama, and we are to leave the estate, and live somewhere else. Pray, do not repeat this to anyone, not until we have... I-It is quite unbearable. From today, I am not a Lady anymore."

"A title is not significant to me, my dear Charlotte. Do not fret about such things. I only require you to be happy once again."

"If I have your alliance, then, of course I am happy." Charlotte smiled, feeling a little better to have Anne as her companion still. Perhaps all was not so horrid as she had deemed it to be.

THE NEXT MORNING, Charlotte decided she would not stay with her mother. She did not want to be the reason for her banishment from the estate, and neither should Dollie go. Her mother would understand, and it was for her well-being to not have her here.

"What are you doing, Lady Charlotte?" Dollie asked, walking into Charlotte's bedchamber.

Before Charlotte lay an empty travelling box, and beside it, some clothes.

"Are you visiting someone?"

"No, I... I am leaving, Dollie. After knowing about my true birth, I cannot stay here any longer. I have ruined Mama's life, and I will not cause her more grief. Perhaps if I am gone, Lord Fallow will come back to live here, and you will also keep your position."

Dollie led Charlotte to a chair and sat her down.

"You will do no such thing," she said calmly. "I would like you to listen to me. Your Mama loves you very much, more than she loves Lord Fallow. If you left her, she would have no one, and that would be her demise. Let me tell you a story. When I brought you to Lady Fallow, I saw the brightest smile I had seen after such a very long time. She cuddled you straight away, and she would not let me take you away.

"Since then, you have barely left her sight. Lord Fallow stopped loving her since the third stillborn and had already begun to spend days and weeks away. Do not blame yourself for anything, my dear. And as for me, I will move wherever her ladyship and you are. I do not care about my wages. I have some saved up, and if I have lodging and food, I will be able to help her ladyship whenever she requires it."

"Oh, Dollie, you are so kind," Charlotte cried and wrapped

her arms around Dollie's waist. "I will not leave Mama, or you, ever."

"Good," Dollie said with a smile. She looked around the room. "You shall miss the luxury certainly, and I hope it will not be too hard on you."

"I do not care for it, truly... Perhaps I do care for my books," Charlotte smiled sheepishly. "And the dresses."

And they both laughed.

THE DAY ARRIVED when Sybil and Charlotte, with Dollie, moved into the small cottage paid for by Lord Fallow. Sybil was grateful for his act of kindness. She was more grateful that he did not divorce her, and she could keep the title of Lady Fallow for Charlotte's sake.

But she was aware their life would be very different now, which she was ready for. They stood outside their new home, taking in the surroundings. It was quite homey with a small garden of flowers and shrubs in the front. The house was situated before a stream. Sybil had left some of her and Charlotte's belongings back at the estate for there would be no room here for everything, nor would everything be needed. She imagined they wouldn't need any of the elaborate dresses as they wouldn't be attending any parties or balls.

Inside the house, there were three bedchambers, very small to what they were used to. She was allowed to have Dollie and a cook.

"Dollie, are you certain you want to come with us?" Sybil asked her before they left the estate. "My allowance will not stretch far, and you will have to undertake other duties beneath your status. You could obtain a better position elsewhere."

"No, my lady. I wish to be with you and Lady Charlotte. I cannot imagine working for another," said Dollie. "It will be all right. I have some money saved, which will help us if need be."

And so, Dollie set about having the house ready for them. When Sybil tried to help, she was stopped.

"You must rest, my lady. Let me carry on, for it is no bother."

Sybil left Dollie to take charge and went to find Charlotte sitting in the garden on a swing. She looked up to see her approach.

"Are you quite all right, Charlotte? You are awfully quiet."

"I was thinking about how different our lives will be, and I feel relieved. I did not expect it so. When we were at the estate, there was a constant dark cloud above our heads, and I could not figure why that was. What happened in the last few weeks has changed that. I now know why you were always so ill, and I am sorry I was the cause."

"My darling daughter, it was my fault this happened. Nothing was your fault." Sybil sighed. She joined her daughter on the swing and saw the beauty before her. A low afternoon sun glittered on the stream before them and shone on the flowers.

"I believe we will be happy here."

And so, they were. As weeks passed, Sybil's health became better. She smiled more and enjoyed numerous walks in the lane behind their new home. Charlotte seemed relaxed too and enjoyed reading the small selection of books she had brought with her under a cherry tree. Often, they would have a picnic with Dollie, talking quietly about the good times.

CHAPTER 22

"Is that a letter from Dwight?" Sybil asked.

Charlotte dropped the envelope on the table. "Yes, yet another one. I wish he would stop trying to see me, Mama."

"Do not be too harsh on him, my dear. He only wants to be with you, and you know you have my blessing."

"But our lives are so different now. How can I allow him to court me when I am now a commoner. We do not have an estate, and we do not have money. He must understand we cannot be together."

"Dwight is a gentleman, Charlotte. He does not see such things. Do give him a chance, my love. I know you love him, do you not?" Sybil poured them some tea. "And it will make me so happy if you do."

Charlotte sighed. In truth, she wanted nothing more than to be with Dwight, but she simply could not see her way clear to do so.

Dwight had been writing to her since they had moved to the cottage, and Charlotte had avoided writing back to him. She was not worthy of his love. They were very different in status now, and she couldn't let him come down to her standing. She was a strong woman, and she knew what was right and what was wrong. Had it not been for Sybil taking her in, she would perhaps be living on the streets in poverty.

She was glad she was where she was now, and perhaps this was her true identity – to live in a modest house and have a modest way of life. And she had to make Dwight understand it. She must not let her heart dictate over her mind.

Yet Charlotte knew she must write to Dwight. He had said in the letter he would come to the cottage himself if she failed to reply. Perhaps it would be a good idea to show him how they lived, then perhaps he would leave her alone. But a part of her wanted to be in his arms as they conversed into the evening, talking about sweet things. She wanted to be his love…

That night, by the dwindling candlelight, Charlotte sat down to write to him.

Dear Mr. Calverton,

It is awfully nice of you to write to me. Please do forgive me for not replying to all your letters. I will not hide the fact that life at the cottage has been very different. Mama and I are slowly becoming used to this new way of living. I do miss my horse, and I often wonder if he misses me. I have decided to meet you one more time, as you must understand our lives are very incompatible now. Society will talk about you and look down upon you if you are acquainted with me. And I do not want that for you. You deserve so much more. However, I will see you as you wish.

Yours sincerely,

Charlotte

Charlotte sealed the envelope ready to be posted in the morning. She blew out the candle and laid down on her small bed, looking out the window into the darkness. She heard a dog bark in the distance and an owl hoot. Slowly, her eyes closed, and she fell into a wonderful dream of her and Dwight talking and laughing and getting married.

Dwight had not written back, which confused Charlotte. Had he received her message? Would he now leave her be? It surprised her to feel hurt to not receive a letter; she should be happy about it, surely? She moved away from the window, admitting it was useless to wait for the post and picked up her book.

Charlotte was so happy to see Sybil becoming stronger each day. This house did make her feel content, away from the dark shadows of grief and her husband's dismissal. Charlotte couldn't think of Lord Fallow as her father anymore; he was just the owner of the Fallow estate. And that was fine with her.

She settled down on her bed and began to read when there was a knock at the door. She went downstairs to see who it was, and when she did, she was shocked to see Dwight, looking rather dashing. Her heart fluttered.

"May I come in?" he asked with a wide smile.

"Oh my, Dwight. I am surprised to see you here." The words rushed from her mouth. Dwight walked past her, laughing softly. He looked around the small living room.

"Why should you be surprised? You did agree to see me again. This is a lovely little cottage," he commented. "Quite comfortable, I must agree."

"You are being kind. It is nothing like the estate. Will you sit? I will have some tea brought out."

A few minutes later, the cook brought some sandwiches and cakes with tea. But neither Dwight nor Charlotte touched them.

"Charlotte, I continue to feel badly about what happened to your family, and that you have to succumb to such a modest living," Dwight began.

"Why did you come, Dwight? You understand we cannot be together, do you not?"

Dwight took her hands. "I do not believe that. You are always Lady Charlotte to me. I must have you, my love. I cannot live without you. Do you not see that?"

"I have no dowry."

"Oh Charlotte, I do not care for a dowry. I only want you. After we marry, I will have your mother and her lady's maid live with us. You would not be leaving them. And you will not have to fret about money or bills."

Charlotte let go of his hand and walked to the window.

"That sounds lovely," she said slowly. "However, I feel like it all may go wrong. Look what happened to my mother. I am not so innocent anymore. If I marry you, what if I cannot bear children or worse... Look what happened to my mother—I would not be able to bear it if you rejected me." She turned to face him.

"I am not Lord Fallow, and I would never do that to you. Please, do not turn me down, my love. I will leave now to speak with my mother and father to finalize my decision. I will see you again and ask permission from your mother."

Dwight stood by the door and gave her a lingering tender gaze before leaving the house. Charlotte watched him disappear down the short path and get inside his carriage, and then she cried tears of happiness that Dwight wanted her as she was.

"I would like your permission to marry Lady Charlotte," Dwight said to his mother and father.

"You already have mine," said Lord Calverton.

"But you do not have mine," came the curt reply of Lady Calverton. "I have said it before, and I shall say it again. That girl is not a lady and never will be. You will not marry a lowly commoner, Dwight."

"I have declared my love for her, Mama. And I have decided it will be her I marry or no one else. I wish you would understand how I feel. I believe I have always loved her."

Once again, they were all in the drawing room. Dwight felt he was having the same conversation one last time.

"Mama, you will either accept this marriage and Lady Charlotte, or you will lose me. I will move to Germany permanently and never see you again. Is that what you want? Your other son is in America for now, do you want me away from you, too?"

"No," Lady Calverton whispered, her eyes wide in alarm. "Do not leave me. I would not be able to bear it."

"Charlotte and her mother will provide no dowry or a means to live as they should. I will be providing for them now. We shall live in our townhouse if Papa agrees."

Lord Calverton's eyes danced. "Oh, how wonderful it is. Go now, son. Go and propose to the lady you love."

With a triumphant grin, Dwight hugged his father and gave his mother a soft kiss on her cheek. She pursed her lips, but she didn't turn away.

"I am truly grateful," he said and went on his way to see Lady Fallow and Charlotte.

LADY FALLOW, of course, gave her blessing to the marriage of Dwight and Charlotte. They awaited Charlotte's birthday, and then the day finally arrived. They married in a small church with Lady Fallow, Dollie, Anne and her mother, and the Calvertons present, after which a wedding breakfast was arranged.

Charlotte smiled at her husband, unable to believe she was married at last.

EPILOGUE

Two years later

The government hospital was busy with more and more poor patients coming in. There had been an explosion at the match factory; many perished quickly while others were burned badly. Charlotte, hot and tired from her voluntary shift, stayed on. She wanted to help these poor souls who cried out in pain, some of their skin still hot and smouldering from the burns. Charlotte rushed from patient to patient, tending them. She didn't think; she just worked.

One of the other volunteer nurses fainted.

"Marion! Wake up," Charlotte splashed some water on her friend's face. "Here," she said, helping her to a chair brought to them by another nurse, who then left to help a patient.

"I'm sorry, I don't know what came over me," Marion said. "I'll be all right now, let me carry on."

Dr. Smith came over. "You should go home," he said. "You have been here since last night. You are exhausted. And you also, Charlotte."

"It's just the heat in here," Charlotte said. "I'll take some air outside and come straight back. Marion can go home."

"No. I will stay, doctor. Just give me a moment," Marion said.

"As you please. I know there is no use talking you out of it," he said, shaking his head. "But if you feel unwell again, you are going home. Otherwise, you will not be any use to any of us."

Outside, Charlotte and Marion took in the fresh air, enjoying the cool breeze before they went back inside the hot and stuffy hospital. Sadly, many would die today.

"It is almost night," said Marion. "Should you not be going home?"

"I cannot leave the doctor to do the work alone," Charlotte repeated what she had thought about earlier in the shift. "Besides, all those people in there... They need treatment."

Marion nodded in agreement. "Mama wants me to stop volunteering here. She says I bring in bad smells and omens. She would prefer me to be married and settle down, have children. You are fortunate Dwight does not mind you working here."

"I am very fortunate. He is a very kind man, and he understands my desire to be of service here. He spends time with Mama at the cottage when I am here, and I cannot be more grateful to him."

"Why did she not move in with you and your husband when you married?"

"Mama told me this was my new life, and I must build it with Dwight. She is very happy where she is now, and she has Dollie."

"Who is Dollie?"

"She is Mama's lady's maid," said Charlotte. "Dollie has been with us since before I was born. They cannot do without each other. I visit Mama most days if I able to when work does not call me."

Eventually, the two women went back inside to start work once again.

"WHAT IS ALL THIS?" Charlotte entered their dining room, where a lovely spread of meats, fish, cheese, and bread lay in wait. Two single candles were lit.

"I thought perhaps we could eat alone today," Dwight said. "You have had a very busy day at the hospital. And I would like to see my wife without Mama's interference."

It was custom for Lady Calverton to dine with them without appointment. Dwight truly didn't mind, and he also didn't mind if his father joined them on occasion. Lady Calverton had still not warmed up to Charlotte, who was just content if they had cordial conversations or none at all.

"How lovely," smiled Charlotte, picking up her glass of port. "It was a horrendous day."

"I heard the match factory was on fire," said Dwight. "It is the topic of the evening at our office. Those poor people."

"Indeed. I do wish those factories were safer."

"Are you thinking about your younger brother?" Dwight asked.

"Albert told me he had begun working at one of those factories, and it does frighten me. He will not stop because he needs the money. And before you offer him money, he will not take charity."

"Then, I will find him a better position elsewhere that he cannot refuse," Dwight said.

"That is why I love you so much, Mr. Calverton." Charlotte leaned over and kissed him.

"And I love you for your kind heart, Mrs. Calverton." Dwight smiled. "How are your other siblings doing? You have not spoken about them for some time." Dwight cut into his fish and took a bite.

"I received a letter from Duncan. He is working in Yorkshire as a carriage driver, would you believe? Michael is now a footman. Marigold is a housemaid. and Katie and Edith have decided to serve the Lord as nuns and teach young ones at the convent school. We will be meeting again in a few months. Will you come again with me?"

"I would be happy to," said Dwight. "I do enjoy conversing with your other family."

"And how was your day today, my love?" Charlotte smiled as she began to eat.

"The paper is always occupied with new information and news. Sometimes I cannot get away as you are aware. Today was no different."

"I am so happy you bought the newspaper. It is quite a satisfying venture."

It was true. Dwight had left his position as a solicitor with the German company, and with the money loaned by the bank, he bought *Craven News*. It was a solid investment and the newspaper had gone from strength to strength. Lady Calverton did not approve of course, depicting it as a lowly vocation. Lord Calverton took his son's side.

That evening, they ate in mutual appreciation of all that life had brought them. Charlotte ate slowly, cherishing the news she had been given earlier that week. She had visited their family doctor, and he was certain she was with child. This, of course, meant she would have to curtail her volunteer hours, and for such a reason, she was excited to do so. There was a part of her who feared the experiences of her mother, but when she thought logically about it she realized there was no reason she would experience that sad fate.

"What are you smiling about?" Dwight asked her. "You look positively pleased."

Despite her fatigue, she grinned playfully. "I am, my dear husband. And now I shall tell you why."

The End

CONTINUE READING...

THANK you for reading **Giveaway Girl! Are you wondering what to read next?** Why not read **The Workhouse Ward? Here's a sneak peek for you:**

1875, Bethnal Green, London. Grace Delagney shoved the washed sheet through the mangle again. It was half day already, and she was nowhere near where she should be. It was another grey, freezing day, and her hands stung as she plunged them repeatedly into the tub of hot water to take out a washed sheet, ready to put it through the mangle. It was an old machine, which she had to pay to use. It was quite rickety, and sometimes the mangle got stuck. It was then very hard to get it to move again.

Still, it was good enough for her. She had work, so she mustn't grumble. She was lucky to have a place to live, even though it was in the cramped basement of a tenement building. The mould on the ceiling and the walls stank, and most nights the basement became unbearable from the fumes. But they had nowhere else to go. Grace would sometimes take Belva to the staircase where there was some air and have her sleep on her lap, snuggled in a thin blanket, hoping the body heat would keep her warm. Grace would hum a song in the long night and rock her to sleep. When Belva was asleep, she would place her on the floor mat back inside their room, and sleep beside her.

Grace eyed the tub of washing she still had to get through, and her heart plummeted. The last few days had been the worst. She was happy for the work, but she couldn't keep up. The money wasn't much, and Grace wondered how long she would be able to go on like this. Still, she tried to count her blessings. She heard the workhouses were far worse, and she never wanted to go there, or to let her daughter experience such horror.

Grace was not scared of work, not at all, and she made that clear to anyone who thought it was their business to say otherwise. If Grace closed her eyes, she could hear them now, talking in loud tones and ignoring her. Was she that invisible?

"Unmarried and twenty-two. And she has a child. Poor thing, she's only five." Grace had heard the woman who was a friend of her neighbour. She spoke loudly, and Grace was no fool to not know the comment was meant for her to hear.

"Mrs Smith, she will hear you. Keep your voice down," her neighbour, Jane Hancock said. "Grace is a lovely girl, but she has fallen on hard times. Like all of us, don't you think?" Jane Hancock was a kind woman, and Grace was glad she'd befriended her.

Mrs Smith scoffed. "At her age, she should be married by now. And she has a child and no husband. I have no sympathy for such behaviour."

Tears stung as Grace remembered those cruel words. It wasn't her fault her beloved had fled as soon as he'd heard she was with child. She had fallen for his charms, only to be left with child. Even after five years, his betrayal hurt.

Click Here to Continue Reading!

https://www.ticahousepublishing.com/victorian-romance.html

THANKS FOR READING

IF YOU LOVE VICTORIAN ROMANCE, **Click Here**

https://victorian.subscribemenow.com/

to hear about all **New Faye Godwin Romance Releases! I will let you know as soon as they become available!**

Thank you, Friends! If you enjoyed *Giveaway Girl,* would you kindly take a couple minutes to leave a positive review on Amazon? It only takes a moment, and positive reviews truly make a difference. Thank you so much! I appreciate it!

Much love,

Faye Godwin

MORE FAYE GODWIN VICTORIAN ROMANCES!

We love rich, dramatic Victorian Romances and have a library of Faye Godwin titles just for you! (Remember that ALL of Faye's Victorian titles can be downloaded FREE with Kindle Unlimited!)

CLICK HERE to discover Faye's Complete Collection of Victorian Romance!

https://ticahousepublishing.com/victorian-romance.html

ABOUT THE AUTHOR

Faye Godwin has been fascinated with Victorian Romance since she was a teen. After reading every Victorian Romance in her public library, she decided to start writing them herself —which she's been doing ever since. Faye lives with her husband and young son in England. She loves to travel throughout her country, dreaming up new plots for her romances. She's delighted to join the Tica House Publishing family and looks forward to getting to know her readers.

contact@ticahousepublishing.com

Printed in Dunstable, United Kingdom